MAN WITH A GUN

MAN WITH A GUN

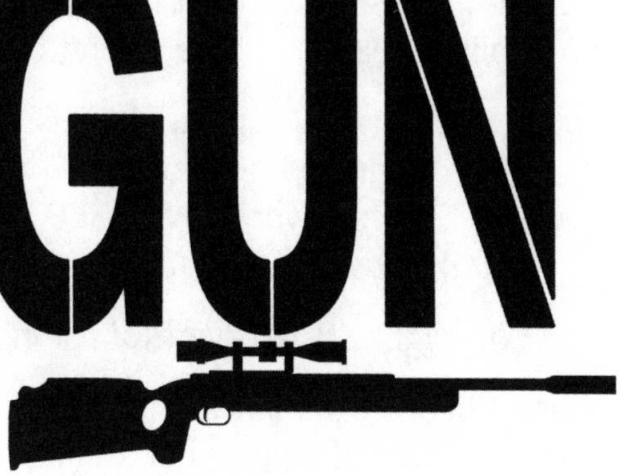

A Tigress Publishing Book

ISBN: 978-1-59404-057-3
Library of Congress Control Number: 2012952224
Printed in the United States of America

Book Design: Steve Montiglio
Editor: Peter Atkins

10 9 8 7 6 5 4 3 2 1

Requests for such permission should be submitted to:
Tigress Publishing
7095 Hollywood Blvd #369
Hollywood, CA 90028

This book is dedicated to all military veterans for they have chosen a life of honor and integrity above all else. They have placed their country's needs before their own and for that I am grateful.

1

The soldier takes some measure of satisfaction
knowing that with the weapon laid out in front of him
he is probably one of the most dangerous living creatures
within a hundred mile radius. Maybe five hundred. Outside
of the city there's an awful lot of uninhabited desert.

He also knows that within a few minutes his life is
going to come crashing down around his ears. And it will
be all his own doing.

For almost an hour now his entire universe has existed
within the one-inch diameter lens of the Unertl scope
perched atop his rifle. There has never been a single time
in his career when, attaching that particular scope, he
hasn't smiled at the fact that it cost more than his first car.
Probably first two combined.

His weapon is an M-40A-3 bolt-action rifle. The cream
of the crop. Lovingly built by United States Marine Corps
armorers in Quantico, Virginia. Accurate to a thousand
yards, it's sixteen and a half pounds and forty-four and a
quarter inches of pure badass delivery. The soldier loves
it more than just about anything he's ever laid his hands
upon.

He's been stationed in Afghanistan for months, but
for whatever reason, at that moment it dawns on him that

he never realized there were so many shades of brown. It is one of those odd thoughts that bloom in the most inappropriate times. From his vantage point on top of the three-story, partially destroyed building fronting the market district of Kabul he has a clear view of every earth tone known to man. His entire universe writ in shades of beige.

At a glance, looking out toward the Hindu Kush Mountains, you can convince yourself you are looking at the Colorado Rockies. Kinda. The soldier feels a strange urge for a Coors Light.

The Colorado reference isn't without merit. Kabul stands almost six thousand feet above sea level. Once he arrived it took the soldier a good couple of weeks to get his wind up to where it should be. Normally a five-mile jog would have hardly made him break a sweat but the first few days up here he felt like he was breathing through a straw. He recalls reading about how an Olympic speed skating training center was built in Butte, Montana. Butte-freaking-Montana! Previously known as the home of a very large hole in the ground, Evel Knievel and a kick ass St. Patty's Day. But the high altitude training worked wonders on Olympic athletes. The soldier could readily testify to the results. He knew when he got back stateside he could make a small fortune sandbagging his buddies with endurance wagers. *Fifty bucks if I can beat you to the top of that hill! Hundred bucks says I can do a sub-five-minute mile!*

But he knew he wouldn't be participating in any such frat boy laughs when he returned. Not after this

2

mission. People at his level of competency didn't get sent to Afghanistan for the regular slap and tickle: rooting out bad guys, whacking the garden variety Mullah. When he was tagged for a mission it was serious shit. And this mission was serious, high methane shit.

The clock inside his head keeps ticking. Not long now. He wonders how he will feel when life as he knows it ceases to exist and life 2.0 begins.

Before he'd taken up position on this particular building he'd been impressed by the sheer size of the city. The mission didn't require needing to know that much about the location but the soldier has always been one for over-learning his lines. He was surprised to learn that Kabul was one of the fastest growing cities on the planet. That it had nearly tripled in size since 2001 and now had a population somewhere between three and five million people, depending on which agency you believed. Either way, a pretty big freakin' city: somewhere near the size of Los Angeles and still growing like a teenager.

He also discovered that only thirty-odd years earlier the place had been relatively stable. Stable in a Soviet-police-state sort of way, but hey, thought the soldier, whatever you might say about the Reds, they kept things orderly. At least until the end of the '70s when they and the Islamic fundamentalists went at it and everything went to hell. That was when the Ruskies sent their troops in when they feared the mujahedeen, the Islamic true believers, might take over. Of course the U.S. had been watching things unravel with a keen eye and had already started moving toward using this opportunity to kick one of the legs out from under Mother Russia. Washington gave the green light for the U.S. military to aid the Afghan insurgents, the Hammer and Sickle got to experience its very own Viet Nam-like seventh circle of hell, and with karma being what it is, it all came back around to bite America in the ass when many of those same U.S. trained and supplied insurgents eventually joined another international pain-in-the-ass organization, the Taliban. Thus endeth the history lesson.

To his right, a second soldier stirs: his spotter. Following an imperceptible movement with his binoculars the spotter whispers into his radio headset. "This is Blue Team. Curtain's up."

A voice on the other end quietly responds, "Roger that. Act one is in play."

The spotter focuses his high-powered binoculars on a nondescript car creeping down the dusty, crowded street, past slow moving animal-pulled carts, buses, bicyclists, vendors and pedestrians. The air is thick with the constantly hovering cloud of dust that picks up the changes in light like a champ. The dust gives everything that soft glow that most Hollywood lighting directors would kill for. The car pulls up to an open space just before the intersection. Its dull paint—a stale, flat gold that may have been all the rage twenty years earlier—is bleached and oxidized from too many days under the sun's hammer and anvil rays.

"Is that a fuckin' Datsun?" The spotter is from Wisconsin so it comes out Daat-sun, with a flat a, like fat or mat. "Don't these rags buy American?"

4

The soldier smiles in spite of himself. Pretty goddamn funny. He follows the same car in his scope. He shifts smoothly into his pre-shot routine. His breathing slows; he lets gravity have its way with his body as he settles in like so much dead weight. The view through the powerful scope gives the impression that the car is mere yards away instead of the quarter mile it really is. His breathing is even, relaxed. He knows no matter how many times you're behind the rifle your heartbeat is going to increase. But you train for that. Your Drill Instructor screams at you at the top of his lungs while you do jumping jacks, push ups and sit ups right before you fire so you're aiming and firing with an active heart rate. Fresh out of sniper school, even with the training, the soldier still would get an adrenaline spike in these situations. Now? Not so much. Four hundred yards? Hell, from that distance he could hit him with his dick.

The car in the scope stops and a nervous looking, dark-complected man gets out. Dark in a purely relative sense. There's that million shades of brown thing again. The soldier suddenly wonders if there's a single tanning bed in the entire country of Afghanistan.

The nervous man is wearing what the soldier has come to consider standard Afghan garb: Perahan Tunban, which literally means 'dress and trousers'. Tan pants, and a dingy green blouse. Baggy, dull and cotton, no matter how you slice it. On his head is a dusty Pakol: a hat that looks like a beret perched on top of a rolled up ski hat. Like a flattened mushroom. This style of dress was more common during the Taliban's regime when anything that even smacked of western culture earned you a one-way ticket to jail. Since the fall of the Taliban in 2001 you saw more jeans and tee shirts but, for many, old habits die hard.

The spotter whispers at him. "You on this?"

The soldier grunts an affirmative. His senses are so heightened at this moment he could have probably heard the spotter whisper from across the street. His body's so quiet it's like it doesn't exist. Right now it's just his weapon and corporeal thought. Everything's on autopilot.

Though sprawled on the exposed rooftop the soldier knows he's virtually invisible. A chopper could be hovering directly above him and he'd probably still go unseen. His BDUs, Battle Dress Uniform, utilized the latest camouflage pattern called MARPAT, short for Marine Disruptive Pattern, which uses a pixel pattern to blend in with the environment. The idea that thousands of miniature rectangles create a superior camouflage always struck the soldier as completely counter-intuitive since nature abhors a straight line. Only Man creates shapes that are perfectly linear. God prefers curves and chaos.

The soldier follows the nervous man as he walks over and meets two other men. Nothing unusual about them, they look like a million other guys in the city: the Afghan version of Smith and Jones. Both dark, one with a patchy beard, the other a mustache, their clothes drab, rumpled, similar to the nervous man's.

The scope pans off the group for a brief moment, doing a quick sweep of the street corner, resting briefly on several other people: a vendor touting his wares, a mother dragging her uncooperative toddler (some things are universal), a teenager with a soccer ball under his arm. The spotter to his right echoes the soldier's move with his binoculars. The quiet, tinny voice quietly cuts in on the spotter's headset. "Blue Team, how we looking?"

The spotter continues his sweep. "Cool at this end. Everything looks five by five." Military-speak for *It's all good.*

The soldier flashes a nasty look at his spotter. A look that pretty much says *Shut the fuck up.* The last thing he needs at this point is unnecessary chitchat. It's distracting and invites radio intercept triangulation. He's not in the mood to be on the receiving end of a counter-sniper team.

The voice at the other end of the radio responds to the spotter. "Roger that. Act Two's coming up."

The soldier's heart makes a tiny hop. The countdown has become official. He feels like he's watching a wrecking ball swinging heavily toward his ancestral home, his own hands on the controls and him still wondering if he really wants to see it all vanish in a crashing roar of splitting timbers and billowing dust.

It's all free will, baby.

The spotter's binoculars return to the nervous man and his acquaintances. Something catches the men's attention and they all turn. The spotter quickly pans over to see another car pulling up to the curb. This one, an ancient Mercedes, equally sandblasted and lacking anything remotely resembling gloss. The spotter cracks a smile. "Bingo."

He snaps his binoculars back as the two men escort the nervous man to the new car that has pulled up. The three men glance around constantly. The car door is opened, but just before the nervous man can get in the spotter hears the soft pop of a silenced round being fired from beside him. Four-tenths of a second later, a quarter mile away, the nervous man's head explodes in a pink mist.

The spotter can only gasp, "What the f..."

It takes several seconds for the people on the street to fully grasp what just happened, but then pandemonium breaks out. Panicked radio chatter can be heard over the spotter's headset, asking for a report, and what the hell just happened. The spotter turns his disbelieving eyes to the soldier next to him. "Do you have any idea what the fuck you just did?"

The soldier quietly stares off into space, a satisfied look on his dusty face. Life 2.0 begins.

2

Webster "Web" Weller paces; the phone to his ear.
"Do you know when he'll return? No, I'm not an agent."
His voice, generally a deep baritone, always level and
measured, is at this moment betrayed by a thin but ragged
edge of frustration. He switches the phone to his other
ear and runs a hand through his shaggy, brown hair. He's
in his thirties but a stranger guessing his age would have
his work cut out for him. Web's weathered, unshaven
face has all the earmarks of early middle age while his
lean, athletic body, impossible to mask, even under the
rumpled, untucked flannel shirt suggests a man many
years younger.

He turns to a soft knock at the apartment door. He
strides over and opens it revealing an elderly woman,
wide-eyed in a floral print house coat and apron, complete
with embroidered rolling pin and "kiss the cook" proudly
displayed across her ample chest. Her grey hair in the
requisite bun, she looks for all the world like central
casting's wet dream of a Toll House cookie commercial
grandmother. A plump hand darts out holding several
pieces of mail, her eyes dancing. "Your mail, Mr. Weller.
I see you got a letter from another publisher. Maybe this
will be the one!"

9

The phone still tucked to one ear, Web gives her a polite nod, and in a practiced motion takes the mail, waves her good-bye and gently closes the door before she can get another word in. He absentmindedly begins opening the letters while speaking into the receiver. "Yes, I understand your publishing company does not accept unsolicited submissions. It's just that...no, I think it's probably a very reasonable policy." One letter after another he opens, glances at and tosses onto a pile on a table in the center of the room; each one a late notice bill. On the last envelope he's rewarded with a paper cut. He jerks his hand away, dropping the traitorous envelope and inspects the nearly invisible but searing little wound. Web wonders how such a tiny little cut can hurt so much. Behold the mighty warrior! Reduced to sucking his finger from a lousy paper cut. Has he really fallen this far? His attention snaps back to the voice on the phone at his ear. "But I think you'll find, if you just give me five minutes of his time that... yes, yes, I understand. Just tell him that I called. Thanks for your time." He hangs up, a tad more forcefully than necessary and continues his pace to the window. He stares out at nothing before collecting himself and returning his attention to the rest of the mail. The paper cut forgotten, he tears open a letter from a publishing company and fishes out the letter. He reads aloud, "Dear Mr. Weller, we are sorry to inform you that your submission, blah, blah, blah..." He crumples up the letter and launches it toward a wastebasket that's surrounded by numerous other balled up letters. The shot bounces off the rim. "Last round draft choice," he murmurs to himself before turning his attention to the final letter. It's addressed to Mr. Nicholas Weller, but is stamped "return to sender" next to the address. He walks over to a shelf, bare except for a single shoebox, Nike Air, size 11. He opens it and places the letter inside, on top of many more identical, unopened letters to Mr. Nicholas Weller, with "return to sender" stamped on them. He gently closes the lid, before returning to the central table and picking up a pad of paper resting there. It's a list of publishers. All but the last one have a line scratched through them. He continues the theme, scratching a line through the last one. He takes a deep breath and looks around the shabby room.

"Screw this."

A half filled duffel bag sits on the scuffed and dusty apartment floor. Probably not the first military duffel to rest there. The three-story brownstone is well into its seventh decade. Many a GI has passed through its rooms. Just the kind of place a guy looks for who just got his walking papers from Uncle Sam: cheap, close to downtown, no long term lease. More a way station than a destination.

Web turns to the mantel above the artificial fireplace and carefully takes down a line of four photos propped there. The first is a classic family portrait, father, mother, two small boys, neither probably more than five years old. The sterile grins suggest they'd just been instructed to say cheese and the photographer had taken a beat too long to snap the photo. The other three pictures are all of two people, the man and one of the boys, the younger, from the family portrait, although over the series of pictures the subjects age at least a full decade.

In the second photo the man kneels beside the boy, who's probably in the neighborhood of seven years old judging by the jack-o-lantern smile, at least two teeth missing; positively glowing with pride, the boy holds up a thin silver trout. Couldn't be more than a pound, but judging by the looks on both their faces they might as well have landed a Great White.

The third photo has the boy, practically swimming in a purple and white football jersey, the shoulder pads comically broad, book-ending his crew-cut head, sitting behind a large trophy, probably a good two feet tall. The man, unmistakably his father with a mirror image buzz cut, sits beside the boy, his muscular left arm draped over the mountainous shoulder pads.

In the fourth photo the boy is leaning more toward manhood. He's well into his teens, his hair shaggier, but the smile still radiant. He and his father, both in camouflage hunting fatigues, rifles cradled in their arms, a four point buck on the grass in front of them, its lifeless head propped up against the boy's kneeling leg. Web lingers over the photos before gently placing them into his bag. He takes down a small, plain wooden box and opens it. Inside are several medals for sharpshooting. Technically they're badges, as they don't have ribbon attached. The three levels of shooting qualification are represented: marksman, sharpshooter and expert. Over the years he's been tempted to throw out the lower badges, the marksman and sharpshooter, but in the end they were always a good reminder of how high he'd climbed in that world. He snaps the lid shut, stuffs this into his bag, shrugs it onto his shoulder and leaves the apartment, not bothering to close the door behind him.

He walks down the chipped, cement steps of the old brownstone. At the bottom of the steps he finds a crumpled five-dollar bill. Even this doesn't rate a smile. President

Lincoln stars glumly back at him. Web mindlessly stuffs the bill in his shirt.

Two blocks later he reaches his car, a 1961 Lincoln Continental convertible that had seen decidedly better days but is still in surprisingly good shape. There's the odd spot of rust on the chrome, and the subtle wave in the paint on the driver's side door suggests it has been on the receiving end of a minor collision at some point where Bondo and sanding can do only so much to hide the effects. Off the showroom floor, the car had been a glowing white, but now the color is closer to used dishwater. The car gives the impression of a middle aged man who takes his daily flaxseed oil and puts in the requisite laps at the local Y but can only do so much to fend off the wages of time. Web steps to the rear and fights with the trunk lock to open it.

While he's cursing his car and fighting the lock three little girls are behind him skipping rope, Double Dutch. The girls are probably around ten years old. Web was never very good at guessing kids' ages. Two are in jeans and tee shirts, probably hand-me-downs from older siblings—brothers, no doubt, judging by the holes in the knees—and the third is in a pale blue knee-length skirt and baggy sweatshirt with Cornell stitched in bold red letters across the front. Web seriously doubts that, in this part of town, anyone in the girl's family attended the Ivy League University. They all wear weathered tennis shoes. Nikes, of course. A girl at each end of the rope, one in the middle, they're trying to do the alphabet, a letter per skip. Baggy sweatshirt keeps tripping up after only a few letters. Web

15

finally manages to open the trunk, tosses in his duffel bag and slams it shut. He stops for a moment to regroup and begins watching the little girls. They switch places and begin again. The new girl does better but not much. She stumbles on the letter G. A thought flashes through Web's mind, racially tinged. He thought all inner city little girls were supposed to be whizzes at Double-Dutch jump rope. At least according to every movie he'd ever seen. It was like it was some kind of ingrained natural ability. Web cocks an eyebrow at this Archie Bunkerish thought, minutely embarrassed. Where's Edith when you need her to slap you upside the head?

Web puts a foot up on the curb, rests a hand on the car's rear quarter panel and nods in the girls' direction. "What's the highest letter you've made it to?"

Baggy sweatshirt says, "J."

Web holds up the five-dollar bill between his fingers, nods at the jump rope. "O." The girls' eyes light up and immediately begin again. They start slow, focused, not wanting to screw up in the first few letters. As they climb higher up the alphabet they hit a rhythm, their speed picks up, the rope becomes a blur as it loops over and under the skipping girl. They make it to Q before they lose synch and the rope tangles around the skipping girl's feet. Web tosses the five dollars on the pavement in front of them. The girls scramble for the money, shrieking the way only little girls do, beyond thrilled. It's amazing what a little motivation can do.

Web hardly cracks a smile.

4

Web pulls up at a deserted military rifle range, deserted except for one soldier who walks out to meet him. He's dressed in olive drab fatigues, billed cap pulled down, shading his eyes, pants ballooning out slightly above where they're tucked into his black high ankle laced up boots. Web gets out of the car and reaches out to shake hands. The man responds in kind with Popeye forearms shot through with bulging tendons. For some reason Web recalls an obscure interview with some old time baseball major leaguer describing the home run king Hank Aaron. How Hank, probably no more than five ten, one eighty and not overly muscular could constantly hit so many monster home runs. The old timer, pointing from his elbow to his wrist, said from here to there no one was stronger than Henry Aaron. Technically Barry Bonds was now the official home run king but to Web it will always be Hammerin' Hank, regardless of what the record books say.

Web shakes hands with the man with only a slight grimace. "Master Gunnery-Sergeant Deke Bedford."

The soldier shakes his head and smiles. "Web, one of these days I'm gonna get busted for lettin' your sorry ass out here."

"I can't exactly shoot at a pistol range, can I?"

"How do you get past gate security? They don't exactly have the welcome mat out for you."

"I have friends in low places. I know you, don't I?"

"That you do. How far you want? 300? 400?"

"500."

Deke cocks an eyebrow. "Right out of the gate. No warming up."

Web turns back to his car, reaches inside and comes out with his rifle. "Table for one. Preferably with a view."

Deke glances up with a dry smile, spits in the dust and wipes his mouth with the back of his hand. "I think we can accommodate you." He turns and heads back to the 500-yard firing line, the one furthest to the back of the range. Web follows. At the line Deke stops, crosses his muscular arms and nods toward the dirt. "Your table, sir. Would you care to see the wine list?" Web ignores him with a smile and kneels down, beginning a weapons check on his rifle. Deke steps back to give him his room "I've already got a target prepared."

"What a nice little piggy."

Deke plants another gob of spit in the dirt. "Your own personal bacon-boy, at your service."

In the sniper world you fall into one of two categories, Pigs and Hogs. Pigs are your *Personally Instructed Gunmen.* Newbies, Probies, guys who haven't yet been to sniper school. Hogs are *Hunters of Gunmen.* Team Leaders, guys who have been through sniper school and can pass along knowledge to the Pigs. Among other low level tasks, the Pigs clean up the hooch, the barracks where the snipers live, and prepare targets for training sessions. Deke is years beyond Pig duty but Web's a friend and he allows the jab.

Web, sprawled out on the ground, the butt of the rifle tucked snugly against his right shoulder, peers down range through the scope. He sees the half mannequin dangling from a hook in the distance. It's just a torso and head, made of high density Styrofoam. More realistic than just a paper target. And what's taped to the front of the mannequin's head gives it the extra touch of realism that snipers demand in their training: a face. Torn out of a magazine, probably an ad for men's cologne. The high-cheek bones, the pursed lips pretty much scream Ralph Lauren. From Web's training experience all sniper targets had a face. They always wanted something you were shooting at to be looking back at you.

Web eases his face away from the scope and raises his right arm up and away from the rifle, rolling halfway over so he's laying on his back looking up at Deke. "Ready when you are, Chief." The Gunny takes his cue and tosses Web his ear protection: large, blue and plastic: like a pair or massive stereo headphones from the early '70s. Both men settle the headphones over their ears. Web returns to his firing position while Deke steps back and takes up a large pair of binoculars that have previously been hanging around his neck.

Web acquires the target and makes a slight adjustment to the elevation knob on the top of his scope. It's a still day, no wind, so he ignores the windage knob to the right of the scope. Wind is a killer: a total pain in the ass for snipers. If for no other reason, the math involved. The formula is pounded into your head in sniper school. You take the range, put that into hundreds, multiply by the velocity of the wind and divide it by a constant. At 175 yards the constant is 14, at 275, it's 13, 375 it's 12, and so on. And people call soldiers dumb grunts. Of course, all your calculations are on the assumption the wind is the same all the way to the target. If it isn't then the math gets even more fun. It makes your brain hurt. Once you get your windage figured you adjust the knob accordingly, which adjusts the compensator inside the scope. Easy-peasy-Japanesie. Easy cuz figuring windage is the spotter's job. Of course the gunman is also doing the math in his head but when push comes to shove the spotter's calculations trump all.

Web squares the reticle, commonly referred to as crosshairs, the two intersecting horizontal and vertical lines in the eyepiece, on a spot just below and to the right of the mannequin's sternum. Along the vertical and horizontal lines in the scope are evenly spaced dots. The dots are referred to as minutes. Because of the distance Web is targeting on the first dot above the center of the reticle. One minute up. The first dot is directly over where the human heart would be in the mannequin. He can see the target is relatively new. Not too many pieces have been blasted out yet.

Everything seems to slow down around him. Web has been asked before what it's like at that moment. The best analogy he has come up with is a basketball player on the free-throw line at crunch time. You don't notice anything else around you; you're completely focused on your target. All you're thinking about is your breathing and squeezing the trigger.

He squeezes the trigger.

He fires off one shot, quickly ejects the shell, fires again, ejects the shell and fires again. It all takes place in about five seconds.

Deke looks down range with his binoculars, then removes his ear protection and glances down at Web as he does the same. "Three shots, three kills, center mass. Go figure."

Web sits up as Deke walks over to him. "I was always under the impression that the Marine Corps wanted to keep guys that could hit the targets."

"Only those who don't reflect poorly on what being a Marine is all about. Didn't you get the memo?"

Web lies back down and begins his pre-shot routine again.

●●●

Web is packing up his rifle. Deke approaches. "What are your plans?"

"You know what I want."

"So you're still bent on playing catch up with Sal Shelby."

Web just shrugs and shakes Deke's hand.

5

Web stands uncomfortably in Sal Shelby's posh apartment. The room is a complete dichotomy to Web: vast and sterile but somehow cozy. He wonders if it's some sort of Japanese Feng Shui thing that goes beyond his feeble human senses. The place is spectacular despite its lack of color or visual warmth. The couch is low, spare, white, and leather, probably the type with an artificial Italian name to boost the glamour factor. It looks about as comfortable as plywood. The armchair is similarly white and misnamed in that it has no arms, a feature Web has never liked. How the hell can you swing your leg up over the arm if there isn't an arm to hang it on? Stupid. The coffee table (glass, natch) balances on a helix of chrome supports. On the spotless walls hang numerous muted paintings, all of a decidedly contemporary bent, undoubtedly worth small fortunes in the world where the ability to create an image that has no basis in real life is apparently considered a virtue. The apartment is impeccably clean and Spartan, virtually no knick-knacks, photos or, god forbid, clutter; like it's inhabited by a monk with very expensive taste. Everything is exceedingly polished, orderly and neat, a mirror image of the apartment's owner who busies himself fixing a cocktail at his wet bar, overlooking a jaw-dropping view of the city. Sal is dressed in what can only be described as casual elegance. Stylish jeans, a crisp white shirt and camel sport coat that no doubt has an Armani or Hugo Boss label stitched into its lining somewhere. Judging by the way everything hangs perfectly on Sal's angular frame, probably not a stitch of the fabric is manmade. Web, on the other hand, with his three-day beard and scruffy clothes, looks decidedly out of place. Web flashes back to an old Sesame Street song from when he was a kid, "*One of these things is not like the other.*" Web feels his mere presence is bringing down Sal's property value.

Web idly wanders over to the one feature of the apartment that is diametrically opposed to the vibe of the rest of the room. On one wall hang weapons. Lots. The one thing that is consistent with the surroundings is that all the weapons are hanging in perfect symmetry. The spacing appears measured to the millimeter, which only enhances the intimidation factor of the display. There are perhaps a dozen weapons of assorted age and make, rifles and pistols, all artfully arranged on a polished mahogany panel, the only warmth or wood in the room to Web's eye. One piece in the collection catches his attention, an exceptionally strange looking weapon. It looks like a double barrel shotgun, except the two barrels go in opposite directions at 90 degrees from the pistol grip.

"What the hell do you call this?

Sal steps over alongside Web. "What you are holding in your hands is one of the rarest guns you will ever find. It's called a Trench Gun." Sal gingerly takes it from Web.

"Supposedly when the user reached a trench he'd reach over the side and bang! Clear on both sides." Sal delicately places it back in the display.

Web shakes his head. "That is seriously messed up."

Sal hands a cocktail over to Web. Amber colored. Scotch and water? Manhattan? No doubt something fashionable. Whatever the cool kids are drinking these days. They touch glasses. Sal gives Web a nod. "Cheers." Web returns the nod and takes a sip. Bourbon and Seven. Decidedly unfashionable, but right on the money, the smoky bourbon blunted by the sweetness of the Seven Up. Like drinking a soda but you still get the buzz. Best of both worlds. Web is silently impressed. Bourbon straight up would have been too stereotypical; would have given the impression that Sal was putting on airs, trying too hard to impress. Web has crossed too many losers bent on emulating the Marlboro Man. Or even the guy on the Bounty paper towel labels. Man's men. Guys who smoke, spit, and throw the word fuck around like it's loose change. Guys who think if booze doesn't instantly dilate your eyes it ain't shit. Mixers are for pussies. Of course guys like that have a tendency to finish their evenings laying in their own puke, going home alone and waking up feeling like twelve miles of bad road. Web has a name for guys like that. Dicks.

Perhaps for all Sal's cosmopolitan trappings he's still the guy Web has known since basic training: Loyal, cocky, outgoing, blue-collar upbringing. The guy more interested in a Pittsburgh Pirates box score than the front page. Of course, Sal was now richer than shit and money can change a person. Web is reading an awful lot into a cocktail.

Salvatore Nicholas Shelby was the only child of Maximilian and Bernice Shelby in Mt. Lebanon, Pennsylvania, a suburb of Pittsburgh. The long held and wholly outdated assumption by anyone outside the Steel City is that if you're from anywhere near Pittsburgh you must have lived a rough and tumble, hardscrabble life while working long hours in a steel mill, your arms and face flecked with scars from flying sparks of molten pig iron. The fact of the matter is that there is no longer a single steel mill within the Pittsburgh city limits, and only two in the county. Pittsburgh is now known more for its technology and financial services, the latter of which is precisely the area of expertise of Sal's dad.

Maximilian Shelby had two profound skills, the first of which was words. The man could strike up and hold a conversation with anyone from a clergyman to a prison guard. He made it a point to know a little bit about everything. He knew that water boiled at 212 degrees Fahrenheit and 373 Kelvin. He knew Rennie Stennet, former second baseman of the Pittsburgh Pirates, went 7 for 7 on September 16th, 1975. He knew that on the *Gilligan's Island* episode where Gilligan must learn to say "Let the prisoners go" in Headhunter-speak, it was "Pulu Si Bagumba." Given the chance Max Shelby probably would have kicked ass on *Jeopardy*. Max also knew numbers. He was one of those freaks of nature who could do long division without a calculator. He knew Pi to the sixth decimal. The guy was the kind of math wiz who'd show up for trigonometry class in high school and say, "A test? Today?" and still ace it. Words and numbers. Separately, those skills were a boon to any businessman. Combined they were lethal. Particularly in the financial industry. Max Shelby knew finance; he knew the figures. He knew the figures so well he couldn't be bluffed or bullied. If he knew a deal wasn't kosher he wouldn't take it. If the numbers didn't add up he simply said no. He made his first million by the time he was 30 and never looked back. At 52, while his son Sal was at baseball practice, an aneurism dropped Max dead over a spreadsheet.

Max Shelby's gift to his son, other than a fat inheritance, was his gift for words. Sal may not have matched the old man's silver tongue, although he wasn't half bad in his own right, but when those words went to paper Sal knew he had a gift. And it didn't take him long to figure it out. By the time he was seven he'd read other kids essays in class and wonder why they were so shitty. He wrote stories in junior high and paid his friends to critique them. He seldom took their advice because they were 14 and idiots but, typical Sal, he knew it made them feel important. In high school he was the editor for his school's newspaper (The Signpost. All the news that's fit to print...and then some). When he graduated he was all ready to be the next big damn deal in the literary world. The only thing in his way was a streak of patriotism that ran one size larger than his ego, which was saying something. The day after he took off his cap and gown he was knocking on the Marine Corp recruiter's door before the recruiter had even warmed up his chair or taken two swigs of his morning cup of Joe. No one could figure out why Sal was so gung ho to Marine up. He was rich, he was talented. Why take a chance that he could end up on the business end of a pissed off Middle-Eastern freedom fighter's sniper scope?

Web was taken by the smooth talking, cocky Shelby right off. And being that they both had a love of writing there was immediate common ground. During basic training they made up their own game where they would try to stump each other with questions about grammar. What's a dangling participle? Can you really not ever end a sentence with a preposition? Not exactly the typical conversation of your typical Marines, but it suited them fine. And being that Sal was so gregarious and Web could light matches with bullets fired from the length of a football field nobody gave them any shit about it.

Web takes a hit off his tumbler and notices there's music quietly playing in the apartment. It takes him a few measures to nail it. Tower of Power's "What is Hip?" Sal was always partial to funky bass lines and tight brass. Web never even noticed Sal picking up a remote or touching a stereo. He's probably got control panels throughout the apartment. Maybe there's a touch screen at the wet bar. Wouldn't surprise him.

Sal fixes Web with a serious look. Serious or sincere, Web had begun losing the ability to differentiate. Over the past several months he'd been on the receiving end of too many of each expression. They've sort of blended together. "Web, I'm really sorry about what you went through. The discharge and all. I'm sure it's been rough."

Sincere. Damn. Web defaults to the reaction he's determined is most appropriate for the empathy; he shrugs.

Sal, still serious, even to the point of looking uncharacteristically uncomfortable asks, "Speaking of which, are you and your dad still...?"

Web cuts him off. "No."

Sal throws up his hands in a gesture of surrender. "Off limits. Understood." Sal then changes tack to try to lighten the mood. "So talk to Sally. What's on your mind?"

Web steps over to the glass coffee table, neatly stacked with several upscale magazines, their edges flush. Who lives like this? It's like the room's been staged for a photo shoot for ADD Apartment Owners Monthly. Web picks up the magazines, fans them out in his hand and slips one from the middle onto the top of the stack. He holds it up for Sal to see. It's an issue of GQ. Sleek, glossy, high quality paper, substantial. On the cover is a photo of Sal, all smiles and veneered teeth. His hands stuffed in his pockets, his sports coat billowing, no doubt from a gigantic fan just off camera, the expression and pose has that pseudo-naturalistic look that can only be captured in a twenty-sixth of a second on the thirty-fifth snapshot. No doubt the photographer and magazine editor sweated over the proof sheets trying to decide between two images that would be considered identical to anyone not studying them through a magnifying loupe on a light table. Web glances back down at the cover. "Nice article. But I have one question."

"Shoot."

"We were both Marines. We both write. Sometimes not half bad." Sal shrugs. Web looks back up at Sal. "Yet you get published in GQ and The New Yorker." Web glances down at the magazine. It sits on his splayed fingers, like a waiter holding a cocktail tray. He's bouncing it slightly like he's trying to gauge the weight. He drops the magazine back on the table with an audible thwack. "And I can't get a publisher to return my calls."

Sal takes a slug of his drink, "Hell, that's easy. I'm great and you suck."

Web responds by flipping him off. Once a Marine...

Sal accepts the bird and moves on. "Seriously, it's pretty simple. Timing and luck."

"That's it? Timing and luck? No skill involved?"

"Okay, a little. Am I a pretty good writer? Yeah, okay, not bad. But after we were in that shit in the Middle East I had something to write about." Sal considers his comment for a beat. "*We* had something to write about. Something most people couldn't even imagine." Sal steps back over to look out at the view, his back to Web. Thirty floors below the city bustles along without a thought. The heat rising up causes the more distant lights to shift and blink. Sal takes in the sight for a beat before continuing. "I happened to be the first grunt to put what I saw into just the right words at just the right time and send it to just the right people." Sal turns back to face Web. "I always thought you were a pretty good writer, Web. Hell, probably better than me, but..."

Web finishes the sentence for him. "But you gotta have a good topic. And you already got dibs on that war."

"I dunno. Seems like there was plenty of war to go around. But I can understand if you'd rather not dredge that stuff up," says Sal. "You can't deny what happened to you would be a great topic." Sal pauses, swirling his drink in his hand. "If, of course, it wasn't classified."

Web responds with a *what-are-you-gonna-do?* tip of the head, takes a sip of his drink and plops himself down onto the sterile white couch. "Holy shit!" Web exclaims even before he knew he was saying it.

Sal, startled by the sudden outburst, rushes over. "What? What is it?"

Web, slumped into the corner of the couch has the look of a man who has suddenly discovered religion. "This is the god-damn, fuckin' most comfortable couch on the whole frickin' planet!"

Sal snorts derisively when he realizes his friend is actually okay and isn't passing a stone or having a coronary. "No shit, Sherlock. Venetian leather. Cost a fortune. Why the hell you think I bought it, asshole?"

Web wriggles deeper into the corner of the sofa. "I want one."

Sal, glad for his friend's approval, brightens up. Back to the subject at hand. "So write something kick-ass and buy yourself one. Speaking of which, how come you haven't sent me an article or manuscript to pass along to my publisher? I'm your in. I'm your guy."

Web continues to wallow in the Venetian leather. "I'd just as soon do it alone. Succeed on my own skills."

Sal shakes his head. "Still the lone wolf, huh? Web, that is incredibly admirable." Sal gives Web a long appreciative nod before poking a finger in his direction. "And stupid. I swear, Weller, you are the most stubborn man I ever met." Sal steps over directly in front of Web. "This business is all about who you know. Take advantage of it, you dumbass." Sal reaches out a hand to pull Web out of the depths of the sofa. Web shakes him off, shifting deeper into the leather.

"I like it here. I do not wish to leave."

Sal doesn't budge, hand still extended. Web finally gives in and takes the proffered hand and is promptly back on his feet.

Web shakes his head and smiles sadly. "If a hack like you can make it, so the hell can I."

Sal returns the smile. "Okay, fine. But promise me that when you find something money, you call me first."

Web answers by raising his glass slightly in Sal's direction, empties his glass in one swallow and sets it down.

With that gesture Sal sees that the end of Web's drink signals their conversation is wrapping up. "Okay, so now what?"

"Gonna get a fresh start."

"Where?"

"Don't know. Just gonna drive west and look for something to write about. Do whatever I gotta do to get published. Make some Web time."

"Road trip."

"Pretty much. Could be a long one."

Sal spreads his arms and looks around his apartment. "Web, I know it looks pretty glamorous, but it's not all it's cracked up to be. There's nothing more frightening than a deadline and a blank page. Besides, it can take over your life. Just ask my ex-wife."

Web reflexively cracks a smile, but it fades almost instantly. He fixes Sal with a dead serious look. He's slipped into mission mode. "Sal, I've sat for days in places so fuckin' miserable it'd make the devil himself puke. Put bullets through the eyes of men and women, watched them drop like a sack of spuds, then went off and had a beer like it was no big deal. Why? Because it was my job. It's what I was supposed to do. And I was good at it." Web picks up his coat. "But putting bullets into bodies isn't the only thing I'm supposed to do in this lifetime."

Sal cocks an eyebrow. "Getting published? Is it really that important to you?"

Web doesn't hesitate. "Yeah." He shakes Sal's hand and heads for the door. Halfway there he stops and turns to face Sal. "You know that blank page you were talking about? Starting today, that's me. And I hope to God it does take over my life, because at this point, I don't have one."

6

The official name of America's Interstate Highway system is the *Dwight D. Eisenhower National System of Interstate and Defense Highways*. The former president championed the cause and successfully made it a reality with the signing of the Federal Aid Highway Act on June 29th, 1956. In typical governmental fashion the initial cost estimate for the highway system was $25 billion over 12 years. It ended up costing $114 billion and taking over 35 years to complete. Along with allowing a convenient means of crisscrossing the country in our automobiles, the Interstate was created for a definite military purpose as well; providing key ground transport routes for military supplies and troop deployments in case of an emergency or foreign invasion. At this moment it's precisely what Web feels like he is experiencing: a deployment; sent off to an unknown land, on a mission.

A popular myth around the Interstate is that one out of every five miles was required to be built flat and straight so as to be used by aircraft for emergency landing purposes. Web knows it's a load of crap. Any pilot worth his salt would be able to land on just about any stretch of Interstate highway should the need arise. Hell, all the pilots Web ever met would tell you they can land their rigs on a ping pong table in a level five twister with their eyes closed while doing the New York Times crossword puzzle in pen. Frickin' Navy and Air Force pukes. Cocky bastards. He likes that.

East-west highways get even numbers, north-south get odd. And of those even numbered I-90 is the granddaddy of them all. I-90 is the longest Interstate Highway in the United States at 3,099.07 miles. It runs from Seattle, Washington to Boston, Massachusetts and wasn't fully completed until 1978. Untold thousands of cars travel this stretch at any given time, but anyone concerned with the overcrowding of America need only spend a few moments on this ribbon of blacktop in the southern reaches of Wisconsin to change their mind. Depending on your general outlook the surroundings fall somewhere between pastoral and serene to lonely and desolate. Either way, uninhabited.

Web's weary Lincoln steams along this stretch with hardly a car passing in the other direction. With his left elbow propped on the windowpane of the driver's side door, his hand posting up his tilting head, he stares blindly into the distance. The radio, volume turned low, more as background noise than for entertainment, quietly broadcasts the local farm report. Something dairy related. The distinct accent gives the only necessary indication of where in the United States he is: Scandinavian territory. Anyone who's watched the movie *Fargo* or has heard his or her share of Sven and Ole jokes knows the accent. You feel you can add *Yah, shore, youbetcha* at the end of any sentence and it would sound perfectly acceptable.

Web shakes off the tedium and blindly reaches around on the expansive leather bench front seat for his miniature tape recorder. He finds it between partially empty bags of Cheetos and scattered cans of Classic Coke. The recorder is weathered, old and held together with gray duct tape. He has to hit the record button a couple of times to make it work. Web speaks into the recorder with a deadpan monotone. "Day three of my great sojourn west. Still looking for the subject of my opus. So far the front runners would have to be Dinosaurland, the World's Largest Pickle and the museum with the three headed calf." He waits a beat. "I strongly suspect there may be better material out there."

Web's Lincoln cruises past a sign welcoming him to the land of ten thousand lakes. He's crossing over from Wisconsin to Minnesota. From where he's sitting there isn't a lick of difference. The ten thousand lakes reference is not an exaggeration. There are 11,842 lakes in Minnesota over ten acres in size. God knows how many the number would climb to if they counted the tiny ones. Right now not a single one of those eleven thousand plus lakes is within eyesight. Around him it's dark, dreary, and unspeakably lonely.

After traveling west along the southern border of Minnesota Web decides to break up the monotony by banking north up highway 35. Before long the distant lights of the twin cities, Minneapolis and St. Paul, begin to lighten the low cloud cover, but the big cities don't appeal to Web; he motors on. Before he hits Duluth and runs smack-dab into Lake Superior he branches northwest onto highway 2. There's neither rhyme nor reason for these decisions, he's going on feel. It's the one thing Web learned to trust more than anything else from his years behind a sniper scope; his instincts.

Before long the landscape changes. The further north he goes the more forested it becomes. He passes a sign: Chippewa National Forest. He likes the sound of it. He motors on through the red oak and white pine. After a mile or two it begins to rain. Hard. Web gives a resigned shake of his head. "Great."

The Lincoln powers on through the sideways rain, leaving an impressive rooster tail in its wake. The odd pair of headlights, their luminance magnified by the downpour, randomly explodes past with a burst of light and sound. Web peers through the rain-streaked windshield trying to see what's ahead but the torrential rain make it a lost cause.

Approximately a mile ahead the noises begin.

The 1961 Lincoln Continental was the first car manufactured in America to be sold with a 24,000 miles or 2-year bumper-to-bumper warranty. Sadly the criteria of that warranty had expired several decades earlier.

After a dozen hours on the highway, the metronomic tone and rhythm of the Lincoln's engine is fused in Web's brain. The sudden and subtle ticking sound jumps out at him like a curse in a convent. With each passing mile the ticking sound grows, soon joined by a rattle, then a sporadic metallic bang, like instruments joining in an industrial symphony.

"Crap."

Web takes out his cell-phone, as beat up as his recorder, and tries to make a call. He dials 411, information. Three rings in, a click, and a female voice asks what she can do for him. Web wedges the phone under his chin to keep both hands on the wheel as the car yaws to the right, hydroplaning on standing water. "Yeah, I'm on highway 2, heading west through Minnesota. I need directions to the nearest gas station. Hello? What? Exit what? What's that?" The phone slips out when he makes a correction with the wheel and bounces off the seat to the passenger side floor. "Shit!" While reaching down to pick it up Web sees an exit come up through the driving rain. He ignores the phone and takes the exit. The road winds off into tall dark trees. Web keeps peering out through the windshield, trying to spot a gas station or store but so far it's deserted. At that moment there's a flash of lightning.

7

Trev Bertrand thinks he has the best job in the world. Swing shift at the local Gas 'n Snack. Most of their customers are daylighters, or as he likes to call them, Eloi, in reference to his most favorite book in the whole wide world, *The Time Machine*, by H. G. Wells. In the classic Wells novel the world is inhabited by two races, the subterranean, dark-dwelling Morlocks, and the aboveground, light loving Eloi. To Trev, all after-hours customers are Morlocks and daytime customers are Eloi. It's his own personal little gag, one that he keeps to himself. He doubts his jackass manager has ever read anything more sophisticated than the sports page and strongly suspects his Eloi reference would be construed as an insult and cost him his cozy gig. The Gas 'n Snack doesn't get much business once the sun goes down. The fact that it's situated a good fifty yards off the road, partially blocked from view until you are practically right on top of it probably has something to do with it. Throw in a general lack of signage on the highway and abject darkness and you have a recipe for low customer turnout. Trev can't figure why they stay open until midnight, they must lose a fortune, but he isn't about to complain. Kicked back behind the counter, surrounded by rows of Snickers, Sudafed, and smelly tree air fresheners (Buck fifty for two!) Trev counts his blessings that he has managed to find a job so completely suited to his needs and station in life. His people skills are limited at best, his goals and ambitions virtually non existent, all he wants to do is hang out in peace and read his sci-fi and fantasy books. He is currently two-thirds of the way through his fifth reading of *The Time Machine*. A stack of paperbacks sits below the counter. Arthur C. Clarke's *Childhood's End* and Ray Bradbury's *Martian Chronicles* are next in line.

8

Web Weller is a fan of science fiction novels as well. His father hooked him on books at an early age. *A book is the best friend you will ever have,* he'd say. *They're always welcome company, and like women, if they ever start to bore you there's a million others more than able to take their place.* Dad always had a way of putting things in perspective.

During Web's overseas tours he passed the time with countless paperbacks. He's particularly fond of Kurt Vonnegut. Vonnegut, too, was a soldier, a POW. Got captured at the Battle of the Bulge. Witnessed the fire bombing of Dresden, up close and personal. Survived it with a handful of other prisoners in an underground meat locker. It was the inspiration for arguably his most famous novel, *Slaughterhouse-Five.* Vonnegut scores double points in Web's eyes: a soldier who became a writer. Way to go, Kurt! Go out and kick Nazi ass and then write a hundred thousand words on time travel and aliens. Web thinks Kurt Vonnegut rocks.

Despite their loner tendencies Web and Trev Bertrand would have probably enjoyed each other's company, talking about their similar taste in literature. But they will never make each other's acquaintance, because at that instance a flash of lightning rips through the darkness. Harmless to Web in his car but not as generous to the transformer two miles to the north, which is at that moment exploding in a shower of sparks, knocking out power within a twelve mile radius. Web drives right by the darkened gas station and never even sees it.

There is something called the Butterfly Effect, in which small, seemingly insignificant occurrences can eventually lead to much greater consequences. For example: a butterfly flaps its wings in Boise, Idaho; a photographer, so enraptured by the insect's beauty and the elegance of its wings, captures the moment in a photo; the photo is published in a national publication; a man who was in witness protection happened to be in the background of the photo; he's spotted in the magazine by someone in New York, tracked down and executed by the mob boss he turned on.

A butterfly flaps its wings, capturing the attention of a photographer, and as a result a man gets a double tap in the head, is stuffed in an oil drum and tossed in the Snake River. The Butterfly Effect. Also know as the "What if?" factor.

That lightning flash is Web's most recent "What if?" moment. What if there was no storm, no lightning and no blown transformer? Web would have probably seen the Gas 'n Snack, would have pulled over, used the phone behind the counter (only for emergencies!) made a phone call to AAA, chatted sci-fi with Trev while he waited and never had to stop in a town called Little Norway.

But he did.

9

Despite the driving rain and enveloping blackness, Web spots a sign looming out of the dark: Entering Little Norway. Population 237. There's a black hole in the white sign, right in the middle of the O in Norway. Bullet hole, no doubt. Web can't blame the triggerman. This is rural country. All signs are free game for rifle-toting locals. Particularly signs with big letter O's on them. They're practically begging to be used for target practice.

A few houses start peppering gaps in the trees, indicating he's entering the early stages of Little Norway. No light glows from any of the homes, their windows like hollow sockets. In daylight they probably appear cheerful and homey, but in the dark and pouring rain they squat grim and lifeless, utterly without charm. He imagines the inhabitants huddled over Coleman camping lanterns or candles, as close to the center of the house as possible where the heat hangs around the longest. Nothing sucks warmth out of a house quicker than a window, open or otherwise.

Web taps on the brakes, slowing the rattling Lincoln, hoping still to spot a gas station or any other sign of life. Seconds later, he's rewarded. Up ahead, a flicker of light. To Web, in this inky blackness, it's as good as a searchlight.

As he approaches he can see it's coming from the window of a small market. Web pulls off the road and eases into the turnaround. It's a stout, one storey job fronted with windows, each crowded with signs touting gun oil, chewing tobacco and Kokanee glacier beer. The light he saw is from a candle in the window. Web stops, gets out into the pouring rain and hurries over to the front door. A small bell attached to the door announces his arrival. Inside, the market is small, tidy and well stocked. Several candles are set around the store giving it a cozy glow. The place looks like a cross between a typical small town market and a military curio museum with assorted framed photos and weapons adorning the walls, windowsills and counters. Two people, a woman and a man, are sitting in chairs along the sidewall quietly talking when Web comes in. The man, if Web had to guess, is probably pushing eighty. Huge weathered hands rest on the knees of his workman's canvas pants that taper into sturdy brown boots, no doubt steel toed. A plaid flannel shirt peeks out from under a heavy camouflage-hunting parka. Thick, salt and pepper eyebrows perch atop small dark eyes that peer out from over veined cheeks that have seen their share of hooch, as Web's dad used to call any and all booze. A green John Deere cap completes the iconic picture.

The woman, trim and angular, appears to be in her early seventies. She's wearing thoroughly worn jeans and a similar patterned flannel shirt. Her gray hair is tied into a ponytail that is long enough for her to be idly toying with it as it hangs down in front of her left shoulder.

Her face, though lined, still has the strong Scandinavian features that age can't erase. A high forehead, nose just slightly large enough to, in her youth, have downgraded her from beautiful to merely pretty. But it's her eyes that capture Web's attention. Blue and riveting. And at that moment trained on Web. The woman politely comes to her feet, moving from the chair with an ease and fluidity that belies her age

"Can I help you?"

Web, normally comfortable around women regardless of age, finds himself feeling like a third grader facing the principal under this woman's intense blue gaze. There's nothing intimidating about her tone, in fact her voice is nothing if not friendly, it's just those eyes are flat out hard to ignore. Distracting, that's the word. He hitches a thumb in the direction of the front door and mumbles, "My car's acting up. Any mechanics in town?"

The woman gives a short nod, seemingly enjoying Web's fidgeting. "I expect." She turns to the old man still seated against the wall. "Bradford, see if you can fetch Pa down here to look at this young man's car." The old man creaks up, unfolding his body from the chair in fits and starts and slowly ambles towards the door. The woman turns her attention back to Web. "What's your name, son?"

"Web Weller."

"Short for Webster, I presume?"

"Yes, ma'am."

"After the dictionary?"

Web's eyebrows do a little hop of surprise and he's

47

trapped back inside the woman's gaze. He says, "How'd you know?"

She gives a shrug. "Only Webster I know. Other than that little black fella on that TV show back in the early 80's. Since it looks like you were born before that, I reckoned you weren't named after him." She extends her hand. "I'm Grace. Grace Ellen Hoolie. I'm the proprietor of this fine establishment, and that there is Bradford J. Pitt. He works over at the meat packing plant down near Yukon, a dozen klicks up the road."

Web actually cracks a slight smile. Not sure if it's because of Grace's military reference or the fact that the crusty old codger's name is Brad Pitt. "Bradford Pitt? Brad Pitt? You ever get confused with the actor?"

The old guy responds with a puzzled look. "There's an actor with my name?"

Grace takes the old man by the elbow and guides him toward the door. "Get a move on, Bradford. It's gettin' late."

The old guy slowly ambles out the door into the darkness. Grace turns back toward Web. "Ol' Bradford knows good and well there's an actor with the same name, he was just funnin' with you. He actually takes a great deal of pride that a fella with the same name is shacking up with a young lady the likes of Ms. Angelina Jolie. He's said on more than one occasion that his younger namesake never woulda had a chance with Angelina if his name was Fred or Larry or somesuch." Grace chuckles at the thought. "Hell, with a face and bod like that his name coulda been Aloysius Farnsworth and he'd still be warming the sheets with any Hollywood hottie he saw fit." She slowly shakes her head. "If only I was forty years younger."

Web nearly snorts in spite of himself.

Grace says, "Speaking of terrible names, did you know there was a Congressional Medal of Honor recipient named Smedley? Smedley Darlington Butler. Received the CMH not once but twice! Only one of nineteen men in history to pull that off. When he died in 1940 he was the most decorated Marine in U.S. history."

Grace rattles off this information like a Gatling gun. "And the crazy thing about Smedley was that he was totally opposed to the actions of the military and he had no problem telling anyone who would listen. Can you imagine? He even wrote a book called *War is a Racket* and considered himself a gangster for capitalism." Grace cracks herself up at the thought. "Oh, Lordy, I'll bet the top brass just about shit a brick every time Smedley opened his mouth."

Grace stops short, eyes wide and slaps her hand to her mouth. "Dang, there I go again. Look at me. I've got this young, good lookin' fella all to myself here in the dark and I go and blow my chances with my potty-mouth. I've lost more men that way, I swear."

Web actually bursts out a fat, round laugh. When was the last time he had a spontaneous happy outburst like that? He can't recall. What he does know is that he cannot help but be impressed with Grace's stream of consciousness ramblings. He has determined this is a woman you could sit next to on a cross-country flight and not be bored for a second. That had always been a litmus test for his mother.

She'd told him on more than one occasion, "If you can't imagine sitting next to them on a flight don't bother with them." Web had taken it to heart. That also might be why he never had too many close friends. There aren't a lot of people he wanted to sit next to for six hours straight.

Grace, enjoying Web's amusement is still wondering aloud about the late-great and unfortunately named Smedley Darlington Butler. "Smedley. Smedley. Hell, even I might think twice about jumping in the sack with a guy named Smedley." Grace gives Web a look that couldn't be more perfectly sincere. "A girl will only go so far, you know?"

Web, completely at a loss before this AARP force of nature in front of him isn't sure if the question is rhetorical or not. He guesses it is and keeps his mouth shut. He must have guessed correctly because Grace powers on without even seemingly to take a breath.

"Smedley. Smedley Darlington." Grace rolls the name around on her tongue like it's fine wine. "Poor kid. No wonder he became a war hero. Probably got his ass kicked at recess so much growing up he figured the only way out was to secure a beachhead or charge a machine gun nest."

Grace locks Web with a potent stare. "How about you? Would you sleep with a girl if her name was Gertrude, Hortense or, I dunno, Bertha?" Before Web can even consider the question Graces smiles and waves away the thought with a flick of her wrist. "Of course you would, you're a man. A guy'll sleep with any girl if she holds still long enough, isn't that right?"

Again with the potential rhetorical question. This time Web opts for holding his hands out helplessly and offers a shake of the head. Uncle.

Grace's historical and ethical ramblings seem to have wrapped up for the moment. She flashes Web an impish grin and walks back behind the counter, set about twenty feet back from the front door. A battered cash register squats on the corner, all brass and stamped black metal. Probably weighs close the same as Web's Lincoln. A box of opened rifle shells sit point-of-purchase just to the side, right next to a small bowl with an explanatory message printed neatly on a card taped to the lip, take a penny, leave a penny. It's currently empty.

Grace slaps her hands on the counter and juts her head forward. "So what else can I do you for this fine evening Mr. Web Weller? Cup of coffee? Power hasn't been out too long. Probably still warm."

Web, never one to turn down a cup of coffee, accepts. "That'd be nice. Thank you."

Grace steps over to an old faded yellow plastic Mr. Coffee maker and pours him a mug. "What seems to be the problem with that boat of yours?"

Web shrugs helplessly. "Beats me. I'm not much of a car guy. That was my dad's thing. He could practically diagnose a problem on sound alone."

Grace grins at Web. "A young man proud of his father. I like you already, Web Weller."

Web shuffles his feet and averts his eyes, again feeling for all intents like an embarrassed eight year old.

"And what is it that you do, young master Weller?"

Web takes the mug in his hands. The coffee must still be pretty warm; he can already feel it through the ceramic. "I'm a writer. Well, trying to be."

Grace theatrically clutches her hands to her chest, like a silent film star. "A writer in our midst! How romantic. No wonder your parents named you after the dictionary."

Web wanders around, glancing at the military knick-knacks, odds and ends. He picks up a grenade sitting on a shelf, the pin still in it. He glances Grace's way.

Grace gives him a sideways tip of the head, "For shoplifters and such."

Web smiles and nods, "That'll learn 'em." He's been in the store for all of five minutes and already has taken a shine to Grace Ellen Hoolie. He can't help but think *if she was only 40 years younger...*

Grace shrugs. "Sorry, I'm a military buff. My weakness. Do you know how they originally determined the height and width of modern battleships?"

"No idea."

"The ships had to be able to go beneath the Brooklyn Bridge and through the Panama Canal."

"No kidding."

"No kidding. Go ahead, try and stump me. Anything military."

"When was the battle of 1812?"

"Smart ass."

"All right. Here's one I think I remember reading in a movie magazine. Why was Paul Newman disqualified from the Navy's pilot-training program during World War II?"

"Ah, my handsome Paul's beautiful blue eyes were colorblind."

"Touché." Web stops in front of an old rifle that's mounted on the wall, looking it over. Just at that moment a truck pulls up outside.

Grace nods toward the door. "That would be your knight in shining armor."

The door opens with a ring of the bell and an elderly man eases in carrying an industrial size flashlight, the kind that can easily double as a billy club. The man's wearing flannel (who isn't?), dungarees and a decades old Minnesota Twins baseball cap. It even has the old twin cities team logo—two identical faces, smiling at each other across a bridge and river, representing Minneapolis and St. Paul. The man in the hat looks to be about the same age as Grace. He shakes off his wet hat and glances Web's way. "Outside. That the rig?"

Grace rolls her eyes. "You know every car in this town, Pa, course that's the one. Patience "Pa" Concannon, Web Weller. Web here is a writer."

Pa holds out a weathered hand. They shake. "Books?"

"Not yet."

Pa's spark of interest promptly wicks out. Web's pride follows suit. Pa then turns and heads back outside.

Web looks skeptically at Grace. "Patience? That's his name?"

Grace nods and says, "No more appropriate name has ever been given a man. You can just call him Pa."

Web and Grace follow Pa outside. It's still raining but not nearly as hard. Pa squints up at the sky, shielding his eyes with a cupped hand at the tip of his hat's brim.

Web glances skyward as well. "Rain's letting up."

Pa just nods and wanders around the Lincoln, looking it over, passing the flashlight beam over from stem to stern.

Web stands back with Grace. "About twenty miles back it started making sort of a knocking sound. Engine started cutting out." Pa just nods and goes about his business. Web continues filling the dead air. "So, you know much about old cars like this?" Pa just shrugs and lifts up the hood. Web's beginning to get a little uncomfortable with Pa's lack of dialogue so he looks over at Grace for help, but she just smiles back at him like everything's peachy. Pa slams the hood back down.

"Reckon I can take a crack at it tomorrow."

Web rubs absently at a non-existent itch on his cheek. "You folks got a motel around here?"

Grace chuckles. "In a town of 237? I'd be happy to let you stay at my place but I'm in the middle of tearing out half the walls. Dry rot. Place is a disaster. How 'bout you, Pa?"

Pa shrugs, waves him over to his truck. "Hop in."

Web, quickly figuring it's accept his hospitality or sleep in the car, grabs his duffel bag out of the Lincoln and throws it into Pa's truck. It suddenly dawns on him that he's been in this town for all of ten minutes and these people are more than willing to allow him, a total stranger, could be an axe-murderer for all they know, into their homes without a blink. Weird. Reassuring, but weird.

Pa looks over at Grace. "Grace, you got that last box of stuff you wanted me to store while you're guttin' your house?"

"Just hold your horses." Grace steps inside the market and appears a second later with a large box, which Pa takes and puts in the back of the truck.

Pa looks at the box skeptically. "This the last of it?"

Grace gives a grin to Web. "I'm a pack rat. Can't bear to throw anything away."

Pa wags his head slowly and grumbles, "Oughta charge a storage fee." Pa climbs into his truck and they pull away into the darkness.

In the truck they drive in silence for a moment before Web takes a stab at small talk. "So, Mr. Concannon, how long have you lived in Little Norway?"

"Call me Pa. All my life. Hell, I was here back when it was a veritable metropolis of a thousand people."

"Grace sure is a nice woman."

"Salt of the earth and sharp as a tack. She try to get you to stump her with military trivia?"

"Yes, sir."

"Sucker." They both trade a smile. "Woman's a walking encyclopedia of military knowledge."

"I can believe it. Her shop is almost like a museum. She's probably the only grocery store in America with a Mannlicher-Carcano bolt action rifle on her wall."

After a particularly long pause, Pa speaks up. "You know your rifles."

"Well, I know enough to know a good rifle from a bad rifle, and the Carcano sure as hell isn't a good rifle. In fact,

I wouldn't even go so far as to call it a rifle. It's a gun."

"Reckon it worked pretty well for Lee Harvey Oswald."

Web just shrugs. "Oswald was ex-military with a scope tracking a slow moving target moving directly away from less than three hundred feet. My grandma could have made that shot." He's silent for a beat. "Even with a crappy gun like a Carcano."

10

They pull up to Pa's small, cabin-like home sitting up on a slight bluff at the end of a gravel road. The windows glow soft bluish-orange from light within. They enter the main room of Pa's house. Web is careful to wipe his feet. The main room has a river rock fireplace a few feet to the left of the front door. A low burning fire crackles. A couple of Coleman lanterns are set around the room giving off a surprising amount of light. That explains the color of light showing through the windows, orange from the fire, soft blue from the lanterns. The place feels like a big, warm hug. From Web's perspective it couldn't appear more comfortable. The room has three raw timber doors on the right, one on the back wall, and a small open kitchen on the far left side of the room. A table sits in the middle. Pa picks up a lantern and shows Web to the door on the far right side of the back wall. Inside is a tiny bedroom with barely enough room for the single bed, nightstand and a cramped table. A window looks out into the darkness. Pa looks around with an ah-shucks nod of his head. "It ain't much."

"It'll do fine. Thanks."

Pa leaves the room and shuts the door behind him.

11

The next morning Web wakes up to a sight he supposes in some circles might be considered normal, but for him, not so much: a girl of about 17 or 18 with a rifle standing in the doorway, watching him. She's tall and thin; her faded blue flannel shirt is three quarters unbuttoned which seems to give her no concern. She watches him with impassive pale eyes. They might be blue, maybe grey. Web's own eyes are still too fuzzy from sleep to register hue; all he can distinguish is shade. He blinks a few times to clear them and offers a bullfrog's hello. The girl backs away out of the room without a word.

Fully awake and dressed, Web enters the main room and crosses over to the table in the center of the room. It's your classic 1950's yellow Formica with chrome legs and trim dulled with age. Four matching yellow chairs surround the table. Web slides one out and takes a seat. A few yards away Pa is making breakfast in the kitchen. The air is thick with bacon and coffee. Web waves his way.

"Morning."

Pa greets him with a warm smile. "Mornin'. Good sleep?"

"Yes, sir."

Pa holds up a long fork skewering a curling, blackened

piece of bacon. "How do you like your piggies?"

Web finds himself getting caught up in the camaraderie and dispenses with formalities. "Browned and bubbling."

"Then you're in luck." Pa hefts a fully loaded plate and strides over to the table.

Web eyes the plates hungrily. "I see the power's back on."

"Yep. Hope you got an appetite." Pa sets the plate in front of Web heaping with pancakes, bacon, eggs; the works. "Flapjacks. Still hot and flappin'. Dig in."

Web doesn't have to be asked twice. One bite and he's pegged Pa for a man who knows from breakfast. He can hardly shovel the food in fast enough. Between bites he nods toward his room. "Who's the girl?"

"Who, Holly? My granddaughter. She just left to help Grace down at the store."

"Where's her father?"

"Dead."

Web mentally whiplashes himself. "I'm sorry." He fills the uncomfortable silence with a few more bites of food. "She always wake people that way?"

"What way?"

"With a gun?"

"Ah, don't mind her none. She just likes guns. Most everyone in these parts has been raised with them. Fact is she's probably the second best shot in town. Kid can hit a quarter from a hundred yards and leave ten cents change."

"Who's the best shot?"

Pa just smiles and winks. Web finishes his breakfast

and looks around the room while Pa continues tidying up the kitchen. Web cleans his plate, gets up and wanders around, glancing at the assorted furnishings. Web stops at a photo on the mantle of Pa in uniform, holding a rifle, from way back when. Next to it is a photo of Pa in his twenties with his arm around an attractive young woman who looks a lot like Grace.

Pa says from across the room, "I gotta get back into town to take a look at that car of yours. You wanna come?"

Web turns away from the photo. "Sure."

12

Web and Pa climb out of the truck outside the market. Pa jerks a thumb toward Web's Lincoln parked a few yards away. "I'm gonna do a little tinkering. You can kill some time inside with Grace. She always appreciates young, good looking men showing her attention and since I'll be tied up I guess that only leaves you."

Web cracks a smile and walks into the market. The hanging bell at the door announces his arrival. Grace is busy putting up a sign for the Memorial Day dinner in the store window. Partially hidden within an aisle, Holly silently stocks the store shelves. Web looks at the sign. It reads, *Memorial Day dinner, this Saturday night, 7pm at the Cabin.* Web wanders over to look it over.

"What's the Cabin?

"It's kind of the town gathering place. Everyone pitched in and built it years ago so they'd have a place to hold all of the town's residents in one place." Web glances over at Holly, but she studiously ignores him. Grace notices the snub and rolls her eyes. "I presume you've met Holly."

"Sorta. So, how many you expecting for your Memorial Day dinner?"

"Everybody."

"Everybody? For Memorial Day?"

"Truth be told about the only time everyone gets together is for Memorial Day and Veteran's Day. That's when we all come together for dinner, then walk down to the cemetery to pay our respects to Little Norway's fallen heroes."

"Had a few over the years?"

"Eight in the great war, fourteen in World War II, four in Korea, three in Viet Nam and one in Iraq."

"That's an awful lot from such a small town."

"That's the price you pay for freedom. Everyone in Little Norway has a good life, and that life is a privilege not a right. What greater honor is there than serving your country?"

Web just nods noncommittally. "I better check back on Pa. He said the carburetor might be shot. I might be here for another day."

"Fair enough. That reminds me, if you're still in town I'll be joining you, Pa and Holly for supper tonight. Once a month we get together for dinner. It's my turn to burn the water."

Just as Web is leaving, a stranger walks in, a drifter: young guy, mid twenties, scruffy. He's wearing black jeans and a well-worn blue denim jacket with a faded yellow patch on his right shoulder. On the patch are smiling green orbs above the words *Give Peas a Chance*—a cartoonish play on John Lennon's famous 1969 single *Give Peace a Chance* that instantly became the theme song for countless hippy sit ins when faced with fidgety cops in riot gear.

The drifter and Holly make eye contact briefly before he turns his attention back to Grace. "Excuse me, ma'am, but could you tell me where I'm at? I mean, what town?"

"This here's Little Norway."

"Little Norway. Huh." The drifter flashes a surprisingly white smile. Pretty good-looking chompers compared with the rest of him: two even rows of little white chiclet teeth. "Well, it's about the most beautiful town I've seen."

Grace fixes him with an overly skeptical look. "Then you obviously don't get out much, my friend." She's half expecting the guy to break into a pitch, trying to sell her a vacuum cleaner or cable service. "So what brings you to our humble little wide spot in the road?"

The drifter's face lights up like a neon beer sign. "Discovering America. Moving from town to town, getting a taste of what this great country is really about." It comes off a little thick, but who knows, some people are just like that.

The drifter buys a pack of gum. Grace rings him up with a bemused smile. Holly continues to steal glances at the drifter. The drifter pockets his gum and wanders about the store, looking at all the knick-knacks. He picks up a dinged up old World War II infantry helmet and looks it over. "You see? This is America! I'd never find something like this in an AM/PM in Minneapolis."

Grace shakes her head tolerantly and tidies up behind the counter. The drifter continues to wander the aisles, but when Grace isn't looking he's pocketing food, a flashlight, batteries. He continues on with his spiel. "Yep, this is the kind of place I've been looking for. A place a fella can really feel like he's part of a community." He and Holly make eye contact. She can see what he's doing and subtly shakes her head 'no', and flashes her eyes back toward Grace. Grace is still busying herself behind the counter, seemingly oblivious to what's going on. She picks up a rag and wipes down the counter.

"Holly, would you be a dear and fetch me another case of beans from out back?" Holly silently nods and obediently walks into the back room. She glances nervously at the stranger. After Holly leaves Grace wipes her hands on the rag and smiles at the drifter. "I'm glad you like it here. Little Norway's a wonderful place, filled with God fearing people." Grace sets the rag down. "But the virtue most people round these parts hold highest is honesty." At this point Graces brings up a rifle from behind the counter and aims it directly at the drifter. She doesn't flinch. "Maybe you're down on your luck, got dealt a bad hand, but regardless, a good man don't turn to thievery." She nods to the rifle in her hand. "This here's a Johnson Arms 1941 .30-.06. Damn fine weapon. Fact is I'm older than this rifle and still have 20/20 vision. Go figure. And if I choose to fire this weapon I will put the bullet right through the third button down from the top of your jacket. Course, the hole in back'll be a might bigger."

The drifter is stock-still. His eyes flash down to the buttons on his denim jacket. Grace nods at the table next to the stranger. He carefully takes each shoplifted item out of his coat and carefully sets them on the table.

Grace gives another nod toward the table. "You can keep the beans."

The drifter carefully picks up the can and places it in his pocket, never taking his eyes off Grace and the rifle.

Grace readjusts the rifle against her shoulder. "Most shopkeepers keep shotguns behind their counters. Wider firing spread, better chance of hitting your target at close quarters." Her eyes never leave the drifter. "But me? For some reason, I'm partial to rifles. Just like the way they feel, ya know? You ever fire a rifle? Course not. You don't strike me as the type. But let me assure you, squaring up the crosshairs on a target and getting ready to pull the trigger...it's better'n sex." The drifter continues his statue act. Grace calmly continues. "Now, if you're still looking to discover America you can find it a few hundred miles due south, just off Highway 5. Norwood Young America, Minnesota, population three thousand five hundred and forty nine." Grace settles her elbows down onto the counter and leans into the rifle more. "And that's about the closest you're gonna get, cuz right here, this ain't America, this here's Little Norway." She nods toward the door. Right before he can take a step Grace steps out from behind the counter and holds up a hand. "Wait a sec." She cross-steps over to a shelf to her left, keeping the gun barrel trained on the drifter. She grabs a can from the shelf and tosses it his way. The drifter catches the can and casts it a nervous, but curious look, then back up at Grace with an even more puzzled expression. She answers him by holding one hand up, two fingers split in the V made famous in the 60's then offers a few words for clarity. "If you don't like the beans...give peas a chance."

The drifter splits.

As the door swings shut Grace wags her head sadly. "No sense of humor."

13

Pa's car diagnosis isn't pretty. The carburetor's not the only thing at death's door. Pa tells Web there's a pretty good laundry list of things cracked, stripped or leaking under the Lincoln's hood. Web's not too surprised. He's never been particularly diligent in the car's upkeep. He's always had more of a fatalistic attitude toward automobile maintenance—it's gonna break when it's gonna break. It is an attitude that never ceased to piss off his old man. Pa goes off into the great unknown in search of parts leaving Web to amuse himself so he strolls back to Pa's house to flip channels. Within a couple of hours the charm of television has grown thin. Web is bored. That always surprises him when it happens. On missions he would spend hours sitting perfectly still and not give it a second thought. Probably because he knew the importance of his role. He was focused. But back stateside with nothing to do he gets itchy.

No one else is home so he wanders about, poking around the main room. When he strolls by Holly's door he pauses. He glances around self-consciously and eases open the door. Inside is nothing like what he is expecting. It's almost like two different people live there. On one wall there are posters of the Eiffel Tower, New York skyline, Golden Gate Bridge while the opposite wall is adorned with several mounted rifles and pistols. Her desk is littered with gun cleaning equipment. A boresnake—a length of thick nylon covered with tiny bronze bristles and a knob of padding at the end, used for pulling through the length of a gun barrel to leave the inside scrubbed and shiny clean—lies strewn across a silicone gun and reel cloth. Assorted brushes and swabs complete the kit. The room has a curious crossbred scent of perfume and gun oil. Roses and machine lubricant. While looking over the handgun that's broken apart on her desk, a Smith & Wesson .22, a good, lightweight hunting pistol for a girl, Web glances at a series of books lined up at the back of the desk; books on hunting, fishing and camping. But he also finds something that's more in line with a typical teenager; a glamour magazine. As Web flips through the magazine, some photos fall out. They're pictures of Holly, obviously taken by herself and probably within the year. They have a surprisingly seductive quality to them. She looks provocative without a hint of effort or force. It occurs to Web it's the first time he's looked at Holly, not just as Pa's granddaughter but as a very attractive young woman. Web gives his head a shake and a reminder. "Jaaaailbait." Web puts the photos and magazine back and slips out of the room.

Just as Web comes back into the main room, the front door opens. It's Grace, Pa and Holly. Grace carries some kind of casserole. Pa happily begins setting the table. Holly slips past Web toward her room. She opens the door, glances in and stops. Her eyes flit to Web, like she might somehow know he was in her room. When Web glances back she doesn't look away, embarrassed that he caught her looking. Her eyes rest on him long enough for him to get uncomfortable. His mind rolls back, turning over what he did in her room, wondering if he left it precisely as he found it. Convinced that he did, he quickly looks to Pa, setting the table, for an escape. "Let me help you with that, Pa."

14

Later that evening Pa, Grace, Holly and Web are well into their meal. Pa and Grace are in good spirits. A bottle of inexpensive red table wine (the house plonk, as Pa called it) sits empty at Grace's elbow. In front of the adults, three wine glasses sit with varying degrees of emptiness. Holly silently eats, occasionally casting furtive glances at Web. Web, even with two glasses under his belt, still feels uncomfortable with her attention. Once again he looks for an escape. "Okay, Grace, which country's army was the last to disband its carrier pigeon service?"

Grace hardly looks up, and talks between bites. "Switzerland. 1996. You're gonna have to do better'n that."

Pa and Holly both look expectantly at Web, seeing how he responds to Grace's challenge. He has no illusions that he's not being judged at this moment. Feeling like a bug under a microscope, he chews slowly and glances up at the ceiling to buy himself a few extra moments to come up with some random piece of military knowledge that the average Joe wouldn't know at the drop of a hat. He's quickly discovering Grace is no average Joe, so whatever he comes up with will have to be pretty damn obscure. He's tempted to make something up but he's certain Grace would call bullshit on him and then he'd completely lose face.

His mind races while Grace, Pa and Holly patiently wait him out. It's clear they're thoroughly enjoying putting him on the spot, but he'll be damned if he's going to let them get the better of him. Growing up, he used to take a lot of pride in his knowledge of trivia. That was another one of the reasons he and Sal had hit it off, being that Sal's dad was such a deep well of useless information. Web flips through his mental rolodex of fun facts he used to stump his buddies with but they all seem to be sports, movie or TV show related. But perhaps one of those subjects has a cross-reference to some military angle. There's something there, he can feel it on the tip of his tongue but he can't quite reel it in. A TV show, an actor, what was it? No, not an actor, a comedian, but who? And then it hits him, George Carlin, he who defined the seven dirty words you can't say on television. Mr. Social Satirist himself. The man who made a career out of taking stabs at political idiocy, the English language, religion, you name it. Nothing was off limits to the man. He was a professional boat-rocker; he was anti-war and anti-authoritarian, that's why this one piece of information got lodged in Web's head in the first place. George Carlin was not the type of person you would expect to voluntarily enlist in the military, but, by God, that's exactly what he did in 1956. Web inwardly smiles. He had it. No way Grace was going to have military knowledge of the Hippy Dippy.

Careful not to look overly sanctimonious, he turns

to Grace and throws it out there. "In which branch of the U.S. military service did comedian George Carlin enlist?" Web makes sure to put extra emphasis on the word *enlist*, just to give the knife a little extra twist.

Grace turns a genuinely surprised look to Pa, who just shrugs and chews. Grace turns to Holly, who returns the glance with her own look of *how the hell should I know?* Grace turns back to Web and nods sagely, dabbing at the corners of her mouth with her napkin. "Well, I must say I am impressed. That is by far one of the best military trivia questions I have had thrown at me in some time. Congratulations."

Web smiles at the compliment, while at the same time thinking *Take that, Miss Smartypants. You ain't all that, after all.* His smugness lasts all of about five seconds. In other words the length of time before Grace starts speaking again.

"George Carlin enlisted (with emphasis on *enlisted*) in the United States Air Force only to be court martialed three times for insubordination. He was eventually discharged after three years for, well, for being a lousy airman, but was still granted a general discharge. The end."

Web sits there like a piece of furniture, his mouth hanging open like a landed bass. Grace couldn't possibly enjoy his expression any more. She, Pa and Holly burst out laughing while Pa leans over and gives Web a *nice try* pat on the back. Pa takes a sip of wine between chuckles and shakes his head with amusement. "Don't take it too hard, son. When you pitch to Joe DiMaggio, you're gonna get hit."

Grace reaches across the table and puts a well-meaning hand on Web's. "Actually, Web, you threw one right in my wheelhouse. Celebrities-in-the-military is probably my favorite subset of military trivia. Did you know that Jimi Hendrix was in the Army? Lasted all of 13 months, and from what I hear he was a deplorable marksman. Couldn't shoot straight to save his life. Eventually got discharged after he broke his ankle on a paratrooper training exercise."

Grace takes a swig of wine, swooshes it around in her mouth a second, swallows and continues. "Remember Don Adams? Get Smart? Nearly died from malaria on Guadalcanal. Steve McQueen, Mr. Cool himself, was a Marine who was demoted seven, count 'em, seven times. Even spent a month in the brig for going AWOL to see a girl, God love him. He did eventually salvage his military career by saving five other Marines during a training exercise. But probably my favorite military celebrity is none other than Scotty from Star Trek."

Web cocks his head, genuinely curious. "Scotty? Really?"

Grace nods. "Really. The man, other than being ridiculously handsome, was a flat-out, dyed-in-the-wool, honest-to-goodness war hero. Charged the beaches of Normandy with the Canadian contingent. Juno beach. Led his men through a minefield, took out two German snipers I'm told. During the invasion he himself got shot all to hell. Four in the leg, and three in the hand that cost him a finger. Go back and watch a few episodes, middle finger gone, he hides it well. He also got shot in the chest but a silver cigarette case deflected the bullet and probably saved his life." Grace slaps her free hand down on the table. "Now that's what I call a man! How d'ya like them apples?"

Web can only shake his head in amazement. "How the hell do you know all this stuff?"

Grace throws back the last of her wine. "Growing up in Little Norway, one has a tendency to have a lot of free time on one's hands."

Web smiles at this. "I can believe it. But you know, I like the slower pace around here. The quiet. It's almost like Little Norway seems to be lost in time. It's so peaceful." Web takes another bite of casserole. "I don't suspect you have much crime around here."

Pa says, "Oh, now and again. A few years back ol' Bradford Pitt caught some fella breaking into his house."

This piques Web's curiosity. "What happened?

"Got what was coming to him."

Web waits a beat for further explanation but Pa leaves the silence untouched.

Graces fills the void. "That reminds me, a young fella came through today, tried to steal some food from the shop, but I sent him on his way." Holly keeps her eyes riveted to her food during this.

Pa smiles. "Didn't shoot this one, did ya?"

Grace waves him off, good-naturedly. "Oh, heavens no. Just made sure he understood that his type wasn't welcome round these parts. Said he was trying to discover America."

Pa asks, "What'd he look like?"

Grace waves her fork in a lazy circle. "Oh, you know, scraggly hair, kinda scruffy. Jeans, jean jacket, cute yellow patch on his shoulder. You may have seen him coming out of the store when you two were fiddling with Web's car."

Pa grumbles. "Didn't see him. Sounds like one of them damn hippies from the 60's."

Web shakes his head and grins. "I can't imagine there were many hippies around here in the 60's."

Pa takes a bite, chews thoughtfully. "If there were any foolish enough to show their faces they'd a left just as quick with a tail full of buckshot for their troubles."

Web looks at both Grace and Pa. "I was too young to really appreciate what was going on in the 60's. Heck, I wasn't even born until the late 70's. It's funny; to me the 60's were never much more than Jimi Hendrix and the Beatles. When you're a little kid the political stuff doesn't really register."

Pa points an empty fork at Web. "You're better for it. I had a front row seat watching America go to hell in a hand basket. All that free love, drugs and those damn Viet Nam war protests."

Grace gives Web a mischievous smile, "Nothing wrong with the free love part," while Pa casts a disapproving glare.

Web says, "My dad served in Viet Nam, the tail end. Were you there too? Wait, you were probably too old."

Pa squints his irritation at the mere notion. "Hell no, I wasn't too old. I was lucky. Served three tours."

Web scrunches up his face in puzzlement. "How is serving three tours in Viet Nam lucky?"

Pa takes a bite of casserole, takes his time answering. "Cuz I survived." Web can only nod to that while Pa continues. "For years I've been listening to these pathetic bleeding hearts blather on about what an unjust war it was. How we shouldn't have been there in the first place. Well, let me tell you something. That's a crock." Pa takes another bite. He's chewing like he's trying to give his jaw a workout. You can see his temperature rising. "It was an honorable war and if we'd been allowed to fight without having one arm tied behind our backs we would have won."

Web tries to mollify Pa. "Well, from what I remember in school, if Kennedy would have had his way from the get go you all would have been out of there nearly ten years earlier."

Pa bristles at this. "Kennedy?! He was the single worst thing that ever happened to the U.S. military."

Grace puts up a hand. "Settle down, Pa. I'm sure Web here doesn't want to listen to one of your rants."

But Pa's having none of it. "No, no, I think this young man here needs a bit of a history lesson," he says and turns his attention back to Web. "You ever heard of the oil depletion allowance?" Web just shrugs. Pa pushes on. "The oil depletion allowance, which had been going on for over thirty years at the time, was a slick little bit of legislation that gave big oilmen a huge tax break. In 1963 Kennedy said he wanted to get rid of it. Smart political move, but typical democrat hogwash. Make lots of blue collar Americans happy by stickin' it to the rich fellas. Now suppose he ditched the program? What would have happened?"

Web shrugs. "Oilmen take it in the shorts."

Pa points a finger at him. "Bingo. They lose countless millions. It's simple economics. When the oilmen lose this money how are they going to make it up?"

Web considers it for a second. "Pass the cost along to the customers."

Pa nods. "And what is one of the biggest clients of big oil?"

Web takes a bite. "The military."

"With Kennedy already slashing their budget and the cost of oil threatening to skyrocket, the U.S. military would have been screwed. It'd be like World War II all over again with Rommel and his tanks in the desert and no fuel to get to the fighting."

Web has no answer for this. There's a moment of uncomfortable silence until Grace breaks it. "A perfect time to start the dishes, wouldn't you say? Holly, give me a hand." Holly and Grace get up with their plates and go to the kitchen area to start washing the dishes. Pa and Web chew in silence for a moment before Web makes another effort at small talk.

"I noticed the picture of you on the mantle; the one of you in uniform. What was your rank when you mustered out?"

"Major. How about you?"

Web feigns shock. "Me? Who said I was ever in the military?"

Pa cracks a smile. "Good Lord, son, how stupid do I look? The military questions you been trying to stump

Grace with, the Yes, sirs, No, sirs, the way you make your bed. Hell, I could bounce a quarter off those sheets."

Web just shrugs. Busted. "Where were you stationed? I started off in Texas, Fort Sam Houston, San Antonio. Ever been there?"

Pa shakes his head. "Close. I've been to Dallas, but that was before you were even born."

Grace wanders back over, drying her hands with a towel. "I reckon I've heard enough boy talk for one night. It's time I skedaddled."

Pa gets up and takes his and Web's plate to the kitchen to help with Holly. Web helps Grace on with her coat. While she's slipping into it she quietly remarks to Web, "Sniper?"

Web pauses for a beat and then subtly nods. Then gives her a quizzical look.

Grace nods knowingly. "I've lived around vets all my life, I know the kind. Besides, I see a precision in you that says marksman. Probably a couple of grades higher than marksman, I'd say." Grace notes the apprehension in Web's face. She puts a hand on his shoulder. "Relax, it's a virtue." Grace turns to face everyone in the room. "Pa, Holly, thanks again for a lovely evening. Holly, you're up for cooking duties next month. See if you can make the Jell-O chewable this time around, would you dear?" As Grace heads out the door she quietly comments to Web. "You know something? I kind of get the feeling you're liking Little Norway. You should consider staying on. In fact you should speak at the Memorial Day dinner. I mean, now that you're one of us."

Web smiles at her "one of us" reference. "I think I'll pass on the speaking but I'd be honored to be there."

Grace returns the smile. "Then it's settled. 'Night."

15

The next morning Web steps out onto the front porch, stretching after a good night's sleep. It dawns on Web he's slept better here than he has in months. A low fog hangs over the tops of the trees, effectively throwing a blanket of silence over the landscape. Web can't believe how peaceful it is. Pa's also on the porch, busily but quietly cleaning his rifle. He gives Web a warm smile. "Morning."

Web stifles a yawn and shivers in the welcome morning chill. "Good morning."

Pa goes on with his cleaning. "When I was working on your car I saw you were still packing your rifle case. I couldn't help but peek. Fine looking weapon."

"Thanks. So's yours."

Pa nods his thanks and continues with cleaning his rifle. Web just stares out across the territory. They're both enjoying the silence. Web finally breaks it. "Say, do you happen to have an almanac or something that has some information about the area? I'd kind of like to get to know it better."

"Hell, Grace'd be better than any almanac. But yeah, I think there must be something like that back in my storage room."

Web nods toward the back of the house. "Is that

where you've been storing Grace's stuff? The room next to mine?"

"That'd be it. There's a couple of boxes full of books near the back. One of them might have what you're looking for."

Web goes inside the house and walks over to the door in the far, back right corner of the main room. Inside, the storage room is a riot of clutter. There's an old 8mm movie projector set up in the middle of the room and a screen propped up at the far end. Web winds his way through the clutter to the back of the room where there are several boxes strewn about. He randomly picks one and opens it up. He does a cursory search before moving on to the next. This box is crammed with books and assorted pieces of memorabilia. He reaches in and takes out an autographed baseball. He looks hard at it to read the faded signature.

"Harmon...Killebrew. Nice." He puts back the ball, signed by the Twins baseball legend, and continues picking through the contents of the box. After a moment he hits paydirt: a small, dog-eared paperback titled *My Minnesota, Mile by Mile* by Vern Nickerson. Web plops himself down on a vacant space on the floor and flips open the first page, reading aloud to himself.

"Welcome to the Land of Ten Thousand Lakes. Explore the exciting international attractions like the Mall of America." Web cracks a smile at this, muttering to himself, "Only in Minnesota can a mall be considered an international attraction." With the book in his hand he peers back inside the box, his curiosity piqued. "What other junk you got in here?" He digs around, pulling out and inspecting a couple more obscure knick-knacks. A gaudy, reticulated 1974 Spokane World's Fair plate, complete with colored transfers of the Fair highlights: Washington State Pavilion, Ride Over the Falls, Oriental Gardens, Skyway Safari, and, in the center, an overview picture of he fair. There's also a small stack of Minnesota Vikings football cards, circa 1976, wrapped in a decaying rubber band. Web tries easing off the band but it disintegrates in his fingers. He fans through the cards: Fran Tarkenton, Chuck Foreman, Mick Tinglehoff. Web squares up the stack and places it back inside the box. While putting it back something else catches his eye: It's a portion of a train ticket, but the only pertinent information on the remaining part of the ticket is the destination, Dallas, and the arrival date, November 21st, 1963. There are also a couple of film canisters with the letters D.P. written on them and a photo of a woman. It's the same woman from the picture with Pa on the mantle, the woman who looks like a younger version of Grace. Placing the canisters and photo back in the box, Web is startled by Pa's voice from the door.

"You find what you're looking for?"

Web absentmindedly jams the train ticket into the almanac like a bookmark and turns to face Pa. He holds up the book. "Think so."

Pa gives an acknowledging nod. "I was about to go out, do a little shooting, just for fun. Care to join?"

Web scrambles to his feet and dusts himself off. He unobtrusively pushes the box behind a larger stack with the toe of his boot. "Sure. Holly coming too?"

If Pa notices anything concerning the box he gives no indication. He gives a nod toward the back of the house. "She's already gone. Out there in the woods somewhere, hunting, hiking, who knows what with that girl. You ready now?"

Web stuffs the book into his coat pocket. "Saddle up."

16

Pa and Web stroll through the lush Minnesota forest, their rifles cradled professionally in their arms. The air is crisp, practically brittle, chillier than normal for late spring but it doesn't seem to faze Pa. He's local and anything above forty degrees is toasty warm. Web is no stranger to chilly temps but even he was expecting the day to be a bit warmer than it is. A few vigorous rubs on his rifle arm give him away.

Pa flicks him a look. "Cold?"

Web considers giving a tough guy denial but scraps it. "A bit. Shoulda brought my heavy coat. Is it normally this cold this time of year?"

"Nah. Just a snap, I expect. Usually it's pretty nice around this time."

"What are your summers like?"

Pa gets a smile on his face looking out over the endless green countryside. "Gorgeous. What's nice about Minnesota is you actually get all four seasons. Rainy in the spring, warm in the summer, beautiful leaves in the fall and snow in the winter. We're like a Norman Rockwell painting come to life."

"Yeah, I've heard about your winters. Not sure it's for me."

Pa gives a knowing nod. "Minnesota winters are not for the faint of heart."

Web rises to the bait. "You saying I'm faint of heart?" he says, before seeing Pa's smile. "How cold does it get around here?"

"Pretty damn cold."

"Cold enough to freeze the nuts off a steel bridge?"

"Colder'n a witch's tit in a brass bra. Pardon my French."

Web nods appreciatively. "That's pretty cold."

Pa pulls up short to survey the landscape. "More times than we prefer, the mercury's been known to drop well below zero. I remember one winter where it must have been 40 below for a week straight. Flat out shut down the town. That whole winter was brutal."

Web sets the stock of his rifle down, holding the barrel pointing a safe angle away. With his free hand he points at his nose. "You ever noticed how when it gets around zero your nose hairs freeze?"

"You noticed that too? Weird, huh." Pa smiles at the thought. "They're like little daggers in your nose. Ten degrees above zero? Nothing. But once that temp drops below single digits, frozen nose hair. Like clockwork."

"With all the snow you get around here I'll bet you've seen your share of white Christmases."

Pa's smile breaks wide open. "That I have. I remember one Christmas in particular where it was coming down, flakes as big as quarters. Jacob and me..." His words trail off, the smile fading for an instant, but he recovers quickly, looking back up at Web. "Well, it was a nice Christmas."

Web is about to ask who Jacob is, but Pa jumps back in. "Now, this last winter. Hell, ridiculous. Hardly snowed a lick. In fact, it was hardly cold at all. Almost had me thinking there was something to all that global warming hooey."

Web waits for Pa to finish his thought and isn't disappointed.

"Almost." Pa lets the word hang, then carries on. "Most folks around here reckon it was probably the mildest winter in the last fifty years. I seen some kids walking around in shirtsleeves on a bright, sunny December day. I checked the thermometer. A balmy 57 degrees. Break out the flip-flops. Everyone was calling it *the winter that wasn't*."

There's a break in the conversation. Web drinks in the landscape. He's hard pressed to remember a place this beautiful. Pa notices the distant look in his eyes. "Addicting, huh?"

Web nods. "It's the kind of place you want to share."

"You oughta give your family a call. Bring em on up here."

Web gives a tight grin and looks down at the dirt. "Don't really have any family left to invite."

"I'm sorry to hear that. Nobody? Brother or sister?"

"A brother. Staff Sergeant. He was killed when his Hummer hit an IED."

Pa's mouth tightens and gives a subtle nod of recognition to the mention of the improvised explosive device.

Web continues. "Mom passed. Cancer."

"What about your dad?"

Web takes a breath and purses his lips, like he's considering how to answer. "Well, dad and me, we don't talk much these days. Sort of had a falling out. You know, father son stuff."

Pa gives Web a long look. "You got a sweetheart somewhere pining for you?"

Web gives an embarrassed smile. "I've kind of sworn off women for a while. Least until I can figure them out a little better. The last one kind of freaked out when I wouldn't marry her."

"How come?"

"I was just getting shipped out. Didn't think it was fair to her if I didn't come back. Guess she didn't see it the same way." They continue on a few steps before Web continues. "Took me a couple of hours to pick up all my stuff she threw out the window."

Pa gets a chuckle out of this. "Oh well, you know what they say, a woman scorned."

Web shakes his head. "I think I'd rather face an armored division."

Pa smiles. "I have. Ain't much difference."

Web and Pa pick their way across some rocky terrain and come to a beautiful overlook. They quietly enjoy the view until Pa breaks the silence. "I was a sniper too."

Web continues looking out over the endless trees. "I know. I saw your rifle in the photo on the mantle. Winchester 70?"

Pa nods. "Then we switched over to the Remington 700 during Viet Nam."

"When did you first go over?"

"First time? Before anybody over here had even heard of Viet Nam. Course, that's when the sniper business kind of grew up."

"In sniper school they taught us that in World War II U.S. troops expended something like 25,000 small arms rounds for every enemy soldier killed."

Pa nods. "And that number doubled in Korea. Glad to hear they're still teaching you fellas pertinent information."

Web finishes the thought. "And by Viet Nam, when every soldier had a fully automatic weapon, that number jumped to 200,000 rounds per dead bad guy."

Pa looks squarely at Web. "And then there was us."

Web returns the look. "One shot, one kill. Hell of a lot more economical."

Pa gives a subtle shrug. "Well, technically it came out to I think somewhere around 1.5 shots per kill. 10,000 dead VC, 15,000 bullets."

Web acknowledges with a quiet "Oohrah". They both stare silently out at the beautiful view for a moment before Web quietly speaks up. "I remember how sometimes I'd be in-country with a bad guy in my sights and thinking, "Don't run..."

Pa finishes it for him. "...You'll only die tired."

Web smiles at their sniper humor bonding. "Did you use a spotter in your day?"

"Sometimes. Since I was what you might call a bit of a specialist I usually worked solo. But now and again, when I was called in for a specific mission and if the target was important enough, I'd work as part of a team."

Web just nods. "When you have to be sure."

Pa nods back, then shoulders his rifle and draws a bead on something in the distance. It's a small, scraggly tree, the lone survivor of a rockslide on an opposing hill about three hundred yards away. Other than the tree there's no other growth within a hundred feet: basically a bald spot on the green hillside. Normally Pa would never fire into open country but the tree and its surroundings provide a safe target. Like firing into a gravel pit.

Web glances into the distance, spots the rockslide on the far hill and recognizes Pa's target. "Yep, there's nothing more dangerous than a man with a rifle."

Pa continues calmly looking through his scope. "Except maybe a woman." Pa fires off a round, turns and gives Web a smile. In the distance a bullet shatters into a pile of moss covered rock after exploding a sizable chunk of wood out of a lonely tree.

17

A half a mile away Holly is creeping through the forest, rifle in hand, keeping her ears peeled for any sounds. That was something Pa always stressed: In deep forest go on sound before sight. You'll almost always hear something before you see it. Speaking of which, she hears Pa's gunshot in the distance, but gives no reaction to it. In these parts distant rifle fire is as common as dogs barking in the suburbs. Something closer and quieter is what's got her attention.

She moves stealthily forward through the brush, her neon orange hunting vest at odds with her quiet movements. She spots a break in the trees and steps out into a small clearing where a campsite has been set up. The flap of the cheap, nylon tent opens and the drifter from Grace's store crawls out. He and Holly spot each other simultaneously and each freezes. The drifter speaks first. "Was that gunshot from you?" Holly scrunches up her face like he must be kidding and shakes her head. Looking relieved, the drifter breaks into a subtle grin and goes about picking up branches and twigs for his pathetic fire, which at this point is actually more smoke than fire. "You the welcome wagon?"

Holly holds her ground. "You shouldn't be here."

93

The drifter continues his search for kindling. "But I am. So now what do we do? Are you here to scare me off? With that vest you could pretty much scare anything."

Holly glances at her bright orange vest, like she forgot she was wearing it. "Don't want to be mistaken for a deer by some drunken hunter." She takes a few steps into the campsite, eyes flashing warily about. "You're lucky you didn't come out of Gracie's store with more than just a scare. She'd just as soon pop a hole in you and no one would have been the wiser."

The drifter smiles, "Now I know why no one ever talks about northern hospitality."

Holly slowly circles his camp, keeping her distance and a firm hand on her rifle. She continues glancing about, cautiously. "You here alone?"

The drifter nods, throws another branch on his puny, smoldering fire. "Gracie? The lady from the store? She wouldn't have really shot me over some beans and batteries."

"You don't know Gracie, and you sure as hell don't know Little Norway."

"I seem to be learning more about it every day." The drifter dumps his clutch of twigs and branches into a small pile next to the fire. "You're not going to tell anyone I'm out here, are you? I got a hunch the rest of your friendly little town might take a similar shine to me as your friend at the store."

"Got that right." Holly sizes up his scraggly campsite. "You planning on staying a spell?"

"Not sure." He stops and eyes her. "But I will if you

come back out and keep me company again."

Holly looks him over dispassionately before cracking a small grin. "I got a better idea. You can keep *me* company."

18

Web walks out of his bedroom into the main room
of the house. He's wearing khakis and a freshly pressed
denim shirt. It's as close to a dress shirt as he has with him.
He doesn't want to embarrass himself at the Memorial
Day dinner. He doesn't have to be the sharpest knife in the
drawer to know this is a big deal to folks in Little Norway.
Pa gives him a quick once over. "Look at you! Spiff!"

Web looks back, embarrassed by the praise. "I wish I
had a tie."

"You can wear one of mine." Pa leaves the room for a
second and returns with a dark blue tie; the kind that goes
with just about anything. He hands it over to Web.

Web takes it from him and looks it over. It's an
inexpensive polyester blend. Probably picked it up at JC
Penney in a previous decade, although the width suggests
it's post-70's when ties were as wide as your salad plate.
"Thanks." Web wanders over to a mirror and fiddles with
the tie for a second but can't seem to remember what goes
over and what goes under. He sheepishly glances back
toward Pa. "I'm a little out of practice."

Pa smiles. "Here, let me." He steps over and begins by
gently shimmying the two ends of the tie to their proper
lengths. "It's always a bit tricky tying from the front.

Everything's reversed." He gives Web instructions like he might be teaching a young boy for the first time. "The rabbit jumps over the fence, goes around the tree, and into his hole." He finishes the single Windsor, crisp and tight. Pa steps behind Web and looks over his shoulder at their reflection in the mirror. Web straightens the tie and smiles. Pa looks proud. "Mothers, lock up your daughters." Pa gives him a pat on the shoulder and goes for his coat.

Web continues looking at his reflection, adjusting the tie. The whole spectacle looks odd to him. It's been a long time since he wore a civilian tie but he remembers the moment in vivid detail. The overcast sky, chilled air and wet grass. He remembers how heavy the casket was. In the movies six pallbearers carry caskets around like they're balsa wood but in reality it's a different story. The suckers are heavy. And his mom was so small. Five foot nothing and a buck five soaking wet. If they'd been carrying around a two hundred and fifty pound man inside that box he's convinced someone's knee would have given out, leather soled shoes would have skated on the wet grass and then it would have been a scene straight out of America's funniest videos. Probably gone viral on YouTube as unshaven 20-something geeks forward the link to their friends across office cubicles and laugh it up in the hallways by the copy machine recounting how the pallbearers all fell on their asses as the casket went skidding past the horrified attendees all dressed fashionably in black and navy.

Luckily no such infamy took place. The funeral went smoothly, quietly and by the numbers. The handful of attending friends and relatives were timid and respectful, much like his mother. She would have liked that response: no fuss. It never ceased to amaze Web how implacable she was right up till the day she died. Most people find out they have cancer and it's a six-month pity party, all *Woe is me* and *What did I do to deserve this?* kind of shit. But his mom would have none of that. She had some sort of Zen calm that seemed to radiate out from her. When people would come to visit, outside the room they were all fidgety and nerves. I mean, how do you act around someone who's dying? That's something no one ever teaches you. But once they entered her space, after a few minutes all anxiety and fear left them. It's like her calmness vibe enveloped you. Web used to joke with his mom that he'd determined that her circle of calming influence had a radius of precisely nine feet six inches and that he was planning on marking it off on the floor of her bedroom with chalk so her visitors would know how close they would have to come before feeling the effects. Web would then stand ten feet from her bed and tell her he felt like shit, then take one step forward and tell her he suddenly felt all puppies and rose petals, then step back and feel like shit again. In response she told him to make sure her brother Pete never got closer than ten feet. She said she was still getting even with him ever since he popped the lock on her diary when she was ten and spilled her utmost secrets to half the school during recess. It was a good thirty seconds before she gave Web an exaggerated eye-roll and told him it was okay if Pete crossed the line... if he brought chocolates. That dry humor was only the second most prominent trait passed on from mother to son. The first was that preternatural calm she exhibited in the face of all number of holy shit situations. Being told she had cancer being number one on that list. Web knew that was the main reason he'd become such an elite sniper: his even disposition. A gift from his mom.

Dolores Weller, maiden name Schifaldie (according to her the main reason she wanted to get married: new last name), was a woman chock-a-block full of non-glamorous, but useful talents, at least in Web's eyes. Give her a pound of hamburger and within twenty minutes you were feasting on something you'd swear was decidedly not hamburger.

The woman could pack like nobody's business. She could cram ten pounds of shit into a five pound bag and everything would come out with nary a wrinkle. Before trips she would repack Web's suitcase and through her black-magic packing abilities always found a way to make room for three extra pair of underwear, two pair of socks, and an extra collared shirt (because you never know). Web and his dad referred to it as Dolores Packing.

She had perfect pitch. An irritating gift if ever there was one, at least to anyone who can't carry a tune in a bucket, Web being one of those people. She could hear a song one time and be able to sing harmony by the second stanza. Web asked how she managed to do that and she said *Beats heck out of me, I just hear it.* Web's aborted attempt at guitar back in junior high school must have been sheer torture for his mom with his thousand failed passes at Led Zeppelin's "Stairway to Heaven".

Web's mind returns to the present as his eyes refocus on his reflection. He flattens his tie against his chest with a few strokes and takes a deep, cleansing breath. The sudden reminiscence stirs to mind a question that's been hovering around Web's brain for a few days now. "Pa, what happened to your wife?"

Pa stiffens briefly, picks up his coat and turns to Web. "Oh, she died a long time ago. Accident."

Web nods toward the fireplace. "Is that her picture on the mantle?"

"Yes."

"She looks a lot like Grace."

"She should. They're sisters."

Web can't hide his surprise. Pa smiles at his reaction and waves him toward the door. "C'mon, we better get going before all the punch is gone."

19

The Cabin, as it's known to everyone in Little Norway, looks, for all intents and purposes, precisely like its name suggests, like a big ol' log cabin. The kind you see in travel magazines and think, *Damn, I'd love to stay in a place like that!* Thick, stacked logs stained a golden honey make up the stout walls while the multi-paned windows are framed in dark green cedar trim. It couldn't look more cozy if it tried. A low peaked, deep red aluminum roof completes the picture. From the outside you fully expect, upon entering, to find a huge stone fireplace, bear rugs, rough hewn furniture and a moose head on the wall. Once inside you'd be disappointed, but only just. The requisite fireplace is there but no moose head. It's basically a large open space, like an Elk's lodge banquet hall. A temporary stage is erected at the far end. A wood podium sits center stage flanked by three flags: the stars and stripes, Minnesota state flag and the unmistakable black and white POW flag.

The floor is packed with town folk. Lots of old timers wearing their uniforms and medals pepper the room. It's readily apparent everyone's enjoying the camaraderie. Pa is introducing Web to everyone, and Web, for his part, soaks it up with warm grins and firm handshakes.

Everyone makes a fuss over him. After the dozenth introduction Web excuses himself and wanders over to the punch bowl. He ladles himself a cup and turns to greet Grace who is manning the table. "Hi, Grace."

"Web. Enjoying yourself?"

"Very much."

"Good. I'm glad you could be here."

The two go silent for a moment as they take in the surroundings. Finally, Web breaks the silence with another stab at military trivia. "In a military contract, what item is referred to as a portable, hand-held communication inscriber?"

Grace sips her punch and never takes her eyes off the crowd. "A pencil."

Web smiles and shakes his head. "Grace, I noticed a picture of Pa and your sister."

This gets Grace's attention. She turns to him. "Yes, Pa and my sister were married for a short time. "

"Any kids?"

"They had a son, little Jacob."

Web nods. "So that's who Jacob is, his son."

Grace gets a nostalgic look on her face. "Never seen Pa so happy as he was during those years."

"What was your sister like?"

Grace's face breaks into a wide grin. "Oh, we were quite a pair. I was the country mouse. Helen, my sister, was the city mouse. Or at least saw herself as a city mouse, even though she grew up here in Little Norway. She couldn't wait to kick the dust of this town off her shoes. She always wanted to live in Chicago, Philadelphia or Washington."

Grace refills her punch cup and takes a sip. "She dragged me along for one trip to DC when we were just out of high school. Helen just had a way about her, always the center of attention. We looked similar, but she had charisma to spare. Men couldn't take their eyes off her."

"I can imagine."

"Oh, and she liked the men. Especially the big city power brokers."

Web nods. "What was it that Kissinger said? Power is the greatest aphrodisiac."

"It sure was the case with my sister. She loved being in the middle of the action. And this is where she and I never saw eye to eye. She loved the DC players and didn't care a lick whether they were married or not." Grace looks down at her punch. "If she saw a man she liked, she went after him like a duck on a June bug, damn the consequences." Grace takes on a thousand yard stare. She's somewhere else.

Web pauses for a second. "So that would make Holly your grandniece."

Grace snaps out of her moment. "Yes, Holly's split right down the middle between Helen and me, for good or for evil."

"So how did a country mouse like Pa end up with a woman like Helen?"

"Love makes women do strange things. All the men Helen ever hooked up with knew she was only with them for the short haul and pretty much treated her as such." Grace takes on a much more matter of fact look and tone. "Now Pa, he had a thing for Helen, just like every other boy in town, but he was such a gentleman. Treated her with such respect that even her live-for-the-moment attitude couldn't hold up against that." Grace gives a nod in Web's direction. "Course, it didn't hurt that he was quite the looker himself, back in the day. That, and the fact that he was an up-and-comer in the military. Bit of a golden boy with a great future ahead of him." Grace stares back off into space again. "Maybe Helen saw a prospective General in her future, to boot. Who knows?"

"So they got married."

"Right here in town, two weeks after her twenty-third birthday. You should have seen it, the whole town turned out. It was Little Norway's version of a royal wedding."

"What happened to the boy, Jacob? In Pa's house I see photos of Pa and your sister, but none of Jacob."

"Oh he's got em, lots. He just keeps them put away. Takes them out when he needs to. I don't think he can bear to look at them on a daily basis. Too much hurt."

Web nods understandingly, "Jacob died."

"He and his wife were killed in a car accident when Holly was just a baby. It was their date night. I remember they were so excited to have a kid-free night together. Tire blew out on the highway. Car flipped..." Grace lets the sentence go unfinished. Her eyes drift aimlessly around the room before she snaps out of it. "At any rate, that's why Pa's been taking care of Holly."

Web's about to ask another question but one of the town folk steps up, a middle-aged man wearing too much cologne. Old Spice. "Grace, you're needed over by the stage," he says, and Grace leaves Web standing there with a shrug and a wave. Web watches her go then steps over to refill his punch cup. He glances up and notices Holly standing just a few feet away, watching him. She looks lovely in jeans and a reasonably feminine blouse. She steps toward him, reaches up and brushes a piece of lint or something equally innocuous from his chest. Her direct gaze and lingering touch make him feel immediately uncomfortable.

"Enjoying your first ever Little Norway Memorial Day dinner?"

"Very much."

Holly gets a surprisingly serious look on her face. "It's a big day for everyone. The vets deserve our respect and admiration and this day is the least we can do for them."

"You know something, Holly? You're not like most girls your age."

"*Women* my age."

Web bows deferentially. "I stand corrected."

"So what do you know of women my age? Do you have much experience?"

Before Web can answer he is saved by a man with a cane standing at the far end of the room, ringing his glass with the handle of his cane to get everyone's attention. The room quiets and everyone takes their seats. Web sits between Grace and Pa. Holly sits on the other side of Pa. They all turn their attention to the man with a cane, as he limps to the podium. "Good evening everyone, it's good to see you all here on this special occasion. It's Memorial Day, a day to recognize the men and women who served their country so honorably...and died for their country."

At the word 'honorably' Web reflexively averts his eyes briefly.

The man with the cane continues on in his strong, slightly high-pitched voice. In the church choir he's lead tenor. "Before we begin I'd like to invite Syril Thorson up to the stage to do us the honor of singing the national anthem. Syril?" The crowd applauds as Syril slowly but proudly mounts the steps and turns to face the American flag that stands at the corner of the stage. Syril is easily in his eighties, with pure white hair and a crisp army uniform. Everyone in the room removes their hats, place hands over hearts and is silent. Syril begins.

At 7am on September 13th, 1814, a lawyer named Francis Scott Key watched as British warships finished bombing the hell out of Fort McHenry at the entrance of Baltimore harbor. The flag that flew stubbornly over the walls, indicating the fort had not fallen, measured 30 feet by 42 feet and was the handiwork of Mary Young Pickersgill and her 13 year old daughter, Caroline, who crafted the flag from 400 yards of the best quality wool bunting at a cost of $405.90. The two-foot wide stars and fifteen stripes, seven white, eight red, each two feet wide as well, were still clearly evident once the smoke had cleared. What Mr. Key witnessed throughout the preceding 24 hours (the rockets red glare, the bombs bursting in air) he scribbled down on the back of a letter he had in his pocket and later named his poem "The Star Spangled Banner." One hundred and seventeen years later, on March 3rd, 1931, by way of congressional resolution, the song officially became America's national anthem.

And Syril Thorson sang the hell out of it.

As anyone who has been to a ballgame knows, the American national anthem is a bitch to sing. Ranging a full octave and a half the song tests every singer's chops but on this day Syril Thorson is up to the challenge. For such an old man he still has a strong, beautiful voice. He sings the anthem, back ramrod straight, eyes riveted on the flag. The crowd is respectful and hushed as Syril finishes the final verse. Web turns slightly to see Holly has a tear in her eye. At the close of the anthem, no one applauds, they simply nod their appreciation and everyone sits. The man with a cane resumes his place at the podium. "Thank you, Syril. As you all know, it is our tradition to have members from our community take this opportunity to share with us their stories from when they served our country. Who would like to begin?"

An old Air Force vet stands. His name is Henry Dahlberg. Stout, weathered and bent, he also appears to be close to ninety. Web can see Henry is wearing formal white gloves with his uniform. The man with a cane nods toward Henry. "Henry Dahlberg has the floor. Henry?" Henry takes a moment to collect his thoughts before plunging in.

"I was in my Mustang, the P-51 and the Messerschmitt had shot the hell out of her. We must have been at each other for nearly ten minutes. Now the Schmitt is a tough son of bitch but she can't turn like the Mustang." Several old timers nod their heads, acknowledging a long lost fact that had probably been drilled into them back in flight school. "When she got on my tail I just kept turning.

Hard. Round and round we went, like we were on some giant spinning top." Henry pauses ever so briefly, lost in the memory. When he resumes his voice is quieter, more thoughtful. "I suspect the other pilot must have been pretty young because a seasoned Schmitt pilot knows if he keeps trying to follow a P-51 in a tight turn he's gonna lose. I don't know how many hard turns it took me with that bastard blasting away at me the whole time but I finally got behind him and just let him have it. At eight hundred rounds a minute with a fifty cal from six guns, that's a lot of hardware I was throwin' his way." The crowd smiles grimly, a few voices burst forth, knee-jerk reactions. *Atta boy, Henry! Give him hell!* Henry nods to a few of the voices in appreciation of their support. "I knew I'd hit him but couldn't land that knockout punch. He finally went into a dive and high tailed it out of there. I was running low on fuel so I let him." Henry stops short again and takes a deep breath. "It was right about then that I noticed the smell. When you're in a dogfight you're so focused it doesn't seem like anything else matters outside of keeping that other plane in your sights. You get stubborn..." Henry holds his hands up and slowly peels the white gloves from them, slowly turning them from side to side so everyone can get a good look at the damage done more than a half-century before. "...even when your hands are on fire."

The crowd gives him the kind of applause and adulation usually reserved for heavyweight champs on fight night. Henry slowly works his way back to his seat under a constant barrage of back slaps, hugs and thanks. By the time the crowd has quieted a middle-aged woman has taken up position at the podium. Grace leans over and whispers to Web, "That's Molly Bannion, she made the punch."

Molly is wearing an immaculate white shirt and knee-length navy blue skirt. She has a plump, grandmotherly look to her, even though she's probably no more than fifty. The woman fairly radiates kindness. She smiles gamely, the kind that seems to be more a gesture of good manners than how she really feels inside. To Web it feels like she's more concerned with putting the audience at ease than revealing her true discomfort. He'd seen that look before, many times, and almost exclusively in base hospitals and M*A*S*H units. It's the look medical staff give patients who are in much worse shape than they realize. It's a look Web knew was greatly appreciated by anyone who witnessed it.

Molly begins her story. "We found the little boy lying in a field. He was probably no more than six. A first grader. We could tell by his injuries that he would not last more than an hour, but we knew the road to the nearest camp would take too long so one of the other nurses carried the boy on her back and we trekked cross country. It was a beautiful, sunny day. The mountains overlooking us were stunning. I remember thinking to myself this would be a wonderful place to vacation...if it wasn't a war zone. It wasn't until we got to the camp that we learned by all rights we should have been dead. The four of us had just hiked directly through a mine field."

Molly quietly nods as the crowd again gives thunderous applause. Web is astonished at the level of respect and gratitude the townspeople have for the speakers. As the applause diminishes a third vet, a man in his sixties with a Viet Nam POW patch on his shoulder stands and walks to the podium. Grace again whispers an introduction to Web. "Lem Parker. High school gym teacher. Toughest sucker you're likely to meet. Total sweetheart."

Like the others before him Lem gives no preamble, just dives right into his story. "They told us to keep moving forward no matter what. If you're shot, keep moving until you're shot again. And if you could still move to keep moving until you were shot again."

For the next half hour Web is mesmerized by a seemingly endless number of veterans recounting their remarkable stories: a soldier's terrifying race across enemy lines under withering fire, a Rosie-the-Riveter's captivating account of how she and her friends learned of the war's end and their subsequent Main Street celebration, a POW's agonizing account of a forced march, men dying of heat and thirst and having to lick the condensation off the hulls of metal ships for water.

The man with the cane takes the podium and says they have time for one last story for the evening. Instantly a small, still very fit looking man, even though he's easily in his eighties steps up. Grace whispers to Web, "Erik Christianson" and says nothing more, like nothing else is needed to sum him up. Web watches as the tiny man stands before the podium. When he begins speaking his voice is quiet, but through some acoustical magic of the Cabin's construction is still easily heard. "I'd been separated from my unit during a firefight and got caught in no man's land when a mortar barrage began." As he continues, his voice grows in strength, as if simply speaking the words is a tonic that has some sort of curative power. "I jumped into the nearest foxhole and quickly discovered there was someone already in it: a German." Web is sure that years before, when the tiny man would previously recall the story, the other man in the foxhole wasn't a German but a Kraut, or more likely a fucking Kraut. Web can practically see the little man's jaw muscles tightening on the word *German* as he bows to political correctness and general good manners. "He must have been a deserter. Our rifles were useless in such close quarters so it was a hand to hand struggle in a hole the size of a bathtub." The crowd is silent. All eyes are on the old man. "In such a tiny space your legs don't help much. It pretty much all comes down to upper body strength. I took immense pride in my strength back in those days. I was the arm wrestling champ of our platoon." A few people smile and nod at the memory. "I wasn't very big, but I could lick guys twice my size because of all the years I'd worked on my daddy's farm, bucking fifty pound bales of hay." He pauses and gets a far off look. "It's a peculiar feeling watching another man die inches from your face. You can tell the moment it happens. It's like a light's been switched off in their eyes. They're watching you and suddenly, even when their eyes are still locked on you, they're not watching you anymore. And you wonder what they *are* seeing."

20

The speeches are over and the crowd mills about, greeting one other, showing off medals and ribbons. It's a scene, Web imagines, which has been repeated every Memorial Day and Veterans Day for decades here in Little Norway. There are smiles and tears. Web steps up to Grace and takes her elbow, easing her away from the crowd. He's had an epiphany. "Grace, I have an idea and I want to see what you think of it." Grace just looks at him expectantly. Web excitedly continues. "I want to write a book about everyone's war stories here in Little Norway. What do you think?" Grace's look of curiosity slowly unfolds to a full-fledged smile.

"Web, I think that's a wonderful idea." Grace grabs a few of the vets standing nearby and pulls them over to Web and he recounts his idea. A few of the vets are hesitant, it's not easy dredging up their experiences, despite what Web just witnessed in the Cabin. Before Web can offer any form of argument, Grace steps in. "I understand why some of you may not want to dig up some of those memories. There's not a person in this room that would begrudge you your silence. This is a purely volunteer mission, and as anyone who ever donned a uniform knows you never volunteer." This cracks a smile in the collected vets who all know this military truism. Grace gives them a moment to acknowledge her little joke. She's working the crowd like a seasoned stage actor, knowing which lines you pause after for laughs or applause, and it's having the desired effect, the vets give her their full attention.

Grace locks eyes with each person for a brief moment, giving everyone gathered the impression she is speaking directly to them, individually. "But this is a win-win opportunity. Our new friend here, Web, is a writer of the first order..." Web feels himself blush at the praise, like a student who's been singled out for praise by his favorite teacher in front of the whole class. "...and writing is one of the most noble professions. It is people like Web, our world's storytellers, who are responsible for passing along our failures and accomplishment to future generations. In fact, it was a Spanish poet, a writer, who once said, "those who do not study history are doomed to repeat it." Web can see the surrounding faces nodding their approval. Grace's words, although slightly melodramatic and soapy, are having the desired effect. It's clear she's a born orator and leader. When Grace speaks people listen, and by God they are listening now. She pauses for effect to again give each vet a direct look before finishing with a well worn aw-shucks attitude. "Well, I don't know about the rest of you but if my stories can bring the ugly reality of war home and maybe help persuade a few people to avoid sending young men off to be slaughtered then, by all means, sign me up."

Her gaze circles the crowd, practically daring anyone to disagree with her, but by this point it's unnecessary.

It's clear everyone is on board. The gathered vets draw closer to Web, offering more words of encouragement and promises of participation. Within minutes, word is spreading around the room. The excitement builds. The more they talk, the more people love the idea and talk excitedly about the prospects. Web breaks away from the crowd to see Pa, who's wandered a fair distance away, keeping to himself.

"So what do you think?"

"Ah, who cares what I think. It seems everyone else is already tickled pink with the notion."

"I can't wait to hear some of your stories."

"Ain't nothing worth talking about." Pa wanders over to the punch table, leaving Web a bit puzzled. The man with a cane who was acting as the evening's de facto master of ceremonies sees Web watching Pa and steps over.

"Going to try to get Pa to share his stories for your book?"

"Absolutely."

The man with a cane just shakes his head with a smile. "Good luck getting Pa to open up about his military background. If you can get him to talk you're a better man than I am, Gunga Din."

"Why?"

"Why? Pa was black ops. Classified stuff. I reckon his secrets will die with him."

21

Damned if Trev Bertrand doesn't have an honest-to-goodness friend. Well, friend might be stretching it a bit but Trev'll take it in a pinch. A man gets to know his limitations and Trev knows he's lousy with them. Antisocial? Check. Geek? Check. Smart mouth? Double check. He knows he's not the guy who can light up a room just by simply walking into it and over the years he's become perhaps not totally okay with it but has at least reached acceptance on that score. The fact that someone is actually friendly to him—hell, even notices him—is cause for minor celebration in his book. Fact is, if someone even shows him anything more than common courtesy he can't help but wonder if that person has an agenda. Trev Bertrand is decidedly jaded.

Trev refers to his new acquaintance simply as Dude. Probably because that's how the man always greets Trev when he walked into the store—"Hey, dude, 'sup?" Nothing unusual about Dude other than he's unusually cheerful and chatty. Keeps peppering Trev with questions about his job, what he is reading; not the stuff most folks normally ask a guy sitting behind the counter of an all night convenience store. But it sure as hell seems like the guy is actually sincere in his questions.

The first time Dude came in Trev didn't give him much of a thought other than the guy was a little too cheerful for his taste. But over the next couple of weeks Dude kept showing up, kept making small talk and slowly drew Trev in. Trev has begun to understand what charisma looks like in person. Dude has it in spades. The only weird thing is that Trev has never got Dude's real name. He asked once but Dude so deftly stepped around the question Trev hardly even noticed the question hadn't been answered. Trev also notices Dude is a kleptomaniac. Sure, he purchases a few things with each visit but he also leaves the store with his pockets and sleeves packed with unpaid items. Trev couldn't care less. Trev secretly suspects Dude knows that he knows and that actually makes it a little cooler; sort of their own little unspoken understanding. Trev also notices he never sees Dude pull up in a car; he always appears on foot, and he always shows up at night. Trev figures he must work late and uses the Gas 'n Snack as a quick pit stop before hitting the sack. Either way, he's glad for it. Trev even finds himself looking forward to the random appearances. It's a strange and slightly foreign feeling for Trev—this minor excitement over having someone to talk to. Trev recalls an article he'd stumbled upon in one of the store's countless magazines; it was about how anticipation is a major key to happiness. It basically said people that regularly have something to look forward to are happier and healthier than people who don't. Trev has to admit the proof's in the pudding. He's been practically chipper since Dude showed up. Weird how something as trivial as a glorified acquaintanceship can put a smile on your face.

Trev has never had his heart broken. He's never been in love. Lust, yes, his magazine counter is packed with Maxim, Playboy, you name it. He's become quite the titty mag connoisseur. He's been emotionally disappointed more times than he can count but it's always come from the female species. Starting with his mom. His dad bailed on the family before Trev was old enough to hate him for it but the good Mrs. Bertrand stuck around plenty long. Too long, in Trev's estimation, if you made him place his right hand on a bible. She wasn't a full-blown alcoholic, just the run of the mill boozer and Friday night Trixie at the local watering holes. Trev lost track of the parade of losers he frequently found sitting unshaven at the breakfast table, seldom to make a repeat appearance. Over the years Trev had thrown up a pretty formidable moat around his feelings and seldom did the drawbridge come down. But down it came, complete with welcome mat, for the guy Trev called Dude.

In a few weeks when Dude suddenly stops coming Trev will shake it off like every other past disappointment but this one will have left a mark. To anyone else what Trev and Dude shared would be considered emotionally paper-thin at best and if you told him so Trev would reply with a sincere *Fuck You*. Over time Trev will convince himself Dude moved away or was just passing through. He really never learned much about the man, never dug deep enough to discover whether he was a Boy Scout or a scoundrel. Either way Trev will still count him the rare bird in his life: a friend.

22

The next morning, back at the house, Web drags himself sleepily into the kitchen just as Pa is heading out.

Pa grins at him. "Too much punch last night?" Web just gives a sleepy smile. Pa stops at the door. "Whatcha up to today?"

"Start working on the book."

"Whatever keeps you out of the bars."

"I don't suppose you have a computer, do you?"

Pa shakes his head. "Not yet. Oh, I suppose I'll get one eventually, for Holly's sake if nothing else. Grace has got one down at the market that we use when we feel the need. I'm sure she'd have no problem with you using it."

"I'll ask her about that. It wouldn't hurt for me to pick up a laptop myself."

"Knock yourself out." Pa gives him a grin before heading out the front door.

Web pulls up a seat at the table and pours himself a bowl of bran flakes when he hears the chopping of wood. He carries the bowl with him and walks out the back door to find Holly splitting logs. There is nothing feminine about her at this moment. Dressed in beaten jeans and a heavy work shirt, her movements are measured and practiced; she works with an unmistakable rhythm; there is no doubt she has done this chore a hundred times over and is well into the routine, like a veteran athlete in the middle of a game. She sets the cedar logs on end, turning the grain lines to run away from her, hoists the three foot axe behind her and brings it up, over and down in fast, violent arc. The log accommodatingly splits with no fuss. Web silently watches for several strokes and Holly silently ignores him. After a while Web plops himself down on a wide stump and happily munches away at his bran flakes.

"You know, most teenagers don't get up till the crack of noon."

Holly effortlessly splits another log. "I'm not like most teenagers." Chop. "Nice cereal. Isn't that for old people?"

Web scratches and yawns. "I am old."

Holly halves another log.

Web, with a mouthful of cereal, points at the axe with his spoon. "Be careful with that axe. I don't want to have to answer to Pa if you chop your foot off."

Holly stops and gives him a long look. "You forget, I'm not like one of those fragile little city girls you're used to."

"I'm not saying you're fragile, it's just that a girl your age..."

"Woman. Woman my age."

Web responds with a bite of cereal, but Holly won't let it go. "Don't tell me you're one of those guys."

"One of what guys?"

"You know, the throwbacks who still see women as barefoot and pregnant, speak only when spoken to, pearls, apron and dinner on the table at five; the helpless female who needs the big strong man to take care of her."

Web shrugs, takes another bite, he's enjoying baiting her. He picks his next words for full effect. "Hey, what's not to like?"

Holly buries the head of the axe in a log and strides toward the house. Web sees he crossed the line. "Hey, slow down, I was kidding!" But Holly ignores him and storms off into the house. A moment later she comes out with a rifle.

"Okay, hot shot, let's see how helpless I am." Web smiles a tad too condescendingly. Holly looks out over the surrounding back forty. "Pick a target." Web looks out over the back terrain and points out a tree about a hundred feet away. Holly scrunches up her face with disgust. "You kidding me?" She brings the rifle up to her shoulder, stares down the sight. "How about that knot six feet up." She fires. Dead solid perfect. She turns to Web. "Don't insult me." She sights through her scope, spots a boulder with a small rock sitting on top of it. "The rock on top of that boulder." She reaches into a small nylon bag she'd also brought from the house and takes out a compact spotting scope and tosses it to Web. He looks it over. This is not your typical civilian spotting scope that hunters pack around the woods, it's a Mark 4 Tactical, the official spotting scope of the U.S. Army's Semi-Automatic Sniper System, also known as SASS. Web is very familiar with the scope. He puts the scope to his eye. Spots the rock.

"Looks to be about three hundred yards, more or less."

"Is it more or is it less?"

Web gives her a look before putting the scope back to his eye and reacquires the rock. "Three hundred and five yards."

"Holly stares him down. "Can I go prone?"

Web cracks a smile and raises an eyebrow at her use of sniper jargon. "Prone? Yeah, sure, go prone."

Holly lies down, sights the rock. She continues to talk while she's looking through the scope. "With a three foot barrel, if I move even a sixteenth of an inch when firing, by the time the bullet's traveled three hundred yards I'll have missed the target by more than three full inches. Then there's wind, elevation. If it were more than a thousand yards I'd have to take curvature of the earth into account. Web's patronizing grin slowly fades. Holly continues on. "And then there's the heartbeats." Holly settles in even more. She becomes incredibly still and relaxed. "You want to fire between them." She's perfectly still and quiet for a full three seconds and then she fires. In the distance the tiny rock explodes. Holly slowly exhales and rolls over onto her back, looking up at Web. Web stares at her evenly.

"Pa taught you well."

"Wasn't Pa," Holly gets to her feet. "It was Grace."

Web can't hide his amusement. "Grace?"

Holly gets immediately defensive. "Yes, Grace. One of the greatest shots ever seen 'round these parts." Holly turns and snaps off a shot at a tree, neatly clipping off a branch. "She'd a been a sniper instructor if they'd allowed it back in the day." Holly fires off another shot, picking off an old coke can in the distance. "Pa kept telling anyone who would listen back at Fort Dix that they'd be nuts not to bring her in, that she was the best shot he'd ever seen." Holly snaps off one last round, but this time misses the rock she was aiming at. She turns to face Web. "What, you think shooting a gun is purely a guy thing?" Before Web can answer Holly jumps back in, ticking the reasons off on her fingers. "We've got a lower center of gravity, we're more patient, careful, deliberate. Women are smart enough to avoid hand-to-hand combat and have a high level of aerobic conditioning. We have fewer genetic visual tendencies like night and color blindness. Want some more?" Web is about to answer but she jumps back in again. "Men are overt, women are covert. And most important of all, thanks to our maternal instincts, women have a stronger killer instinct than men." Holly stops, waits for Web's response. Web doesn't crack a condescending smile. Doesn't do anything but return her serious gaze.

Web says, "Women are also overly emotional, carry grudges and can be vindictive. Three things you never want in a sniper."

Holly gives a tight grin, "Don't piss us off. Just sayin'."

Web rises from the tree stump he's been sitting on and walks over closer to Holly. "Did you learn all this from Grace? The walking military encyclopedia?"

Holly cocks her head, kind of like a puzzled dog. "Do you know who Lyudmila Pavlichenko was? She was in the Russian army. Killed over 300 German soldiers." Holly continues to glare at Web, practically daring him to say something. He obliges.

"The actual number was 309." He flips her the spotting scope, turns and walks back toward the house. Then, while walking away, "Using a Mosin-Nagent sniper rifle with a P.E. 4-power scope."

Holly watches him go, offering a respectful grin. Then to herself, "There's hope for him yet."

23

Web sits in the living room of a small, old, but tidy house. The living room shelves are packed with small Hummel porcelain statuettes. The kind you find on the Home Shopping Network and will never see in a home of anyone under the age of seventy. Most of the figures are of small children in assorted poses and expressions of wide-eyed cuteness. Web can see why they're referred to as *collectables* as there has to be over a hundred of the little suckers. There's hardly a flat surface that doesn't have a cherubic little face staring back. Web guesses them to be the passion of the wife of the man he is here to interview. Web can't imagine any man worth his salt has ever bought a Hummel figurine unless it was a gift for a wife or daughter. Web feels slightly redneck-ish at the thought.

Across from him sits Henry Dahlberg, the old vet who gave the story of being in a dogfight with a Messerschmitt. Henry is not wearing his gloves this time. His hands are pink and shiny. Web picks up his dilapidated tape recorder and punches the record button. It won't start. It takes him a few punches to get the thing rolling. He notices Henry's bemused smile. "Sorry, stupid thing's even harder to stop. Earlier today when I was interviewing old Chuck Pernell, down on Erickson Street, I found the recorder never turned off, even after I hit the stop button. Thing just kept rolling until it ran out of tape." He speaks into the recorder. "Interview number four, Mr. Henry Dahlberg." Web sets the recorder down on the doily-covered end table.

Henry gives a nod toward the device. "Why don't you get a new recorder?"

Web shrugs. "Cuz I'm cheap and stubborn."

Henry nods, knowingly. "I'm Norwegian. Same thing." The interview commences.

Henry recounts his story of the dogfight along with a few other aerial battles. After listening to what Henry went through: the bomber missions, the dogfights, flying through clouds of flak, Web can hardly believe Henry is still alive and tells him so. Henry answers with a roll of his bent shoulders and a single word. "Lucky."

24

The interviews go on for days and Web is thoroughly enjoying the process. Each interview, each story, brings him new emotions. Emotions he thought had been lost, or been deadened years ago. Some of the interviewees tell their stories with hardly a blink, as if their horrific circumstances or acts of bravery were commonplace. Others tell their stories in fits and starts, regularly breaking down at the memories. Web is amazed at how some can recall the most granular details from something that happened to them seventy years ago; this from the same people who frequently can't remember where they left their reading glasses five minutes earlier.

The town people obviously like Web and he likes them in kind. They offer him coffee, lunch, and show him pictures and memorabilia. For the first time since he left the service Web Weller has a sense of belonging.

25

Augie Perlman is a small, balding man, perpetually stooped but armed with a mischievous grin. He sits perched on the front lip of his threadbare Barcalounger, sipping from a small demitasse cup. Web's tape recorder sits on a TV tray between him and Augie while Web himself sits on a faded yellow dinette chair, similar to the vintage of the ones in Pa's house. He flips open his notebook. An elderly woman in a faded periwinkle shift watches quietly from the kitchen. Web nods her way, she nods back before Web turns his attention back to Augie.

"So, it's Augie? You spell that with an AU or OGG?"

"AU, just one G, short for Augustus, last name Perlman. I'm the town's token Jew. Gotta give these damn Scandinavians some diversity." Augie flashes a lopsided smile, but after a beat the smile fades. Augie pauses, collecting his thoughts before leaning in conspiratorially toward Web. "I've been waiting a long time to give this interview. Longer than you've been alive." Augie pauses for another moment, seemingly at a loss for words. He seems to be struggling with whether to continue. Web patiently waits him out. After a few moments of indecision Augie seems to come to a conclusion. He nods his head, perhaps more to himself than to Web. "You'll have to excuse my reticence. I very much want to tell you my story but when you've kept quiet about something as long as I have it's not easy to spit it out."

Web nods agreeably. "Whenever you're comfortable."

Augie gives a rueful smile. "No, I don't think I'll ever be comfortable talking about this. You see, Mr. Weller, once I cross this line there's no turning back. If this book of yours gets published then I'm for all intents and purposes dropping my pants for all the world to see. Once the Genie's out of the bottle, he don't go back in. You follow what I'm saying?"

Web is finding himself getting more than a little concerned by Augie's comments. He's wondering if his brilliant book idea was so brilliant after all. He nods dumbly.

Augie looks down at his knotted and veined hands. He flexes them, turns them over, inspecting them, all brown spots and crepe-paper skin. "Funny. When what I'm about to tell you happened to me I was such a young man. Even younger than yourself. Barely out of high school."

Web punches the record button on his tape recorder, double checks it to make sure it's rolling and sets it down between them.

Augie purses his lips and begins. "What I'm about to tell you isn't in any history books."

"Why is that?"

"Because according to the United States military it never actually happened." Augie gives a dramatic pause before continuing. "I was a buck private in the European theater. The war was winding down. The Nazis were pretty thinned out and were hightailing it back to der Fatherland. At least the smart ones." Augie gives Web a knowing glance and takes a sip from his cup. "At any rate, we were all feeling very heroic at the time. We would sweep in like the epic figures we saw ourselves to be at this point in the war and liberate a town. But in this one little town our protocol was different."

"How so?"

"We'd gotten word from one of the leading citizens that the last time the Nazis swept through here they made off with several of the women. Ugly stuff. So, to put their minds at ease, our commanding officer took it upon himself to relocate many of the women, the younger ones in the village to a safe haven until later. Just in case some Nazis returned after we'd left."

"Noble idea."

Augie eases back into his chair. "Wasn't it, though? That's what we thought too. But the problem was...he wasn't really moving the women to a safe place."

Web's eyebrows involuntarily rise in curiosity. He leans in toward Augie, making up the space from when Augie leaned back. "What was he doing?"

Augie lets the question hang in the air for a few seconds before replying. His eyes become distant. "Selling them. Black market. Sex slave traders. Well, maybe not all of the women, but enough of them." He takes another sip from his cup. His hands are shaking. Augie's eyes regain their focus, like he suddenly woke from a dream. "You know how I found out? This." He holds up a tarnished old nickel. "This nickel. You see, I

135

was the old man's driver. I was taking him into town for a meeting with that one upstanding local citizen I was telling you about. The local honcho. So while he's inside, I'm sitting out in the jeep killing time, flipping a nickel. This nickel." Augie sets it down gingerly on the TV tray. "So I'm flipping and catching, flipping and catching... and I drop it. Stupid thing bounces off the fender and rolls around the corner. So I go looking for it and I hear something coming through a crack in the window. It's the old man talking to this fella. I listened, I learned their secret. I heard everything, the whole ball of wax."

Web scratches his head, more to buy a moment to figure out what to say next than to sooth an itch. "Mr. Perlman, uh, that's a pretty incredible story. I gotta say it's also pretty tough to swallow."

Augie fixes him with a bemused smile. "So you're saying I'm a liar?"

Web immediately backpedals. "No, no, it's just that... well, perhaps you misheard what the commander said."

Augie doesn't blink, doesn't become defensive, doesn't even raise his voice. In fact his utter calm is what makes his accusations more persuasive. "No, I didn't mishear the commander. Although I wish I had."

"Mr. Perlman, with all due respect I've never once heard of an American military officer accused, let alone arrested or convicted of something like this. I know it was pretty common with the Japanese army during that time."

"You're talking about Comfort Women."

"Yes. A buddy of mine did a paper about it when he

136

was at West Point. It was shocking. Women rounded up and forced to have sex with soldiers."

"That wasn't the half of it. Trust me, over the years I became quite familiar with the topic of human trafficking during wartime. I've become a veritable poor-man's scholar on the subject."

Augie eases up from his chair and slowly shuffles over to a heavily laden bookcase. Looking down through his bifocals he traces his finger across the spines of several thick books before coming to rest on one: a wide, academic looking tome, dusty blue. He wiggles it free and looks the cover over. He flips it open to the first pages, presumably to the table of contents, and gives it a cursory glance before finding what he is searching for. He wets his finger and turns the thick pages. The book appears well worn. "Ah, here we go, Comfort Women in World War II." Augie's demeanor changes. He's no longer the grandfatherly old man sipping tea in his living room; suddenly he's the wizened college professor tutoring the clueless freshman. "There are no definitive numbers on how many served as Comfort Women during the war. It really depends on whom you ask, the Japanese or the Chinese. Japanese place the number around 20,000, Chinese put it around 400,000."

"Between 20,000 and 400,000? That's quite a discrepancy."

"Most scholars tend to lean more toward the Chinese figure. Hard to imagine but the whole idea of Comfort Women, or in Japanese, "*jugaun ianfu*," was actually a government-approved program. It was given the seal of approval by something called the *Imperial Conference*, which was made up of the emperor, some important folks at the top of the armed forces food chain and the top Cabinet ministers. Started around 1937."

Augie carries the book back to his chair and drops himself back in. After a quick scan he finds where he left off. "The women weren't just Japanese but Chinese, Korean, you name it. Girls as young as 11 years old, many kidnapped and kept at Comfort Stations, which were basically military rape camps."

Augie pauses to remove his glasses and massage his eyes. Web wonders if it's perhaps just to give himself pause from continuing to read the words. But when Augie takes his hand away Web sees no tears, no redness around his eyes. In fact, if anything they are dispassionate. No, that's not quite right. Web can see there's something there, a sadness that's papered over with, what? Resignation? Augie closes the book in his hand, staring softly at Web. "The women were forced to have sex with as many as 50 soldiers a day. They were used until they were too sick to perform or simply died."

"That's horrific."

"Yes. That would be a good word for it."

"I still find it difficult to believe an American soldier, an officer for that matter, could have been complicit in something similar."

Augie actually smiles at this. "What? American military personnel are all upstanding citizens? Abu Ghraib, Guantanamo Bay, Afghani civilian thrill-kills, any of these sound familiar? And that's just in recent history. Sorry son, I'm as proud of our armed forces as anyone but in every barrel there's bound to be a rotten apple."

Web looks down at his notes. "Okay, then, for the sake of argument, after you allegedly overheard the commander..."

Augie smiles and nods. "Allegedly. I like that. Well done." Augie waves in apology for the interruption. He nods for Web to continue. Web waits a beat before continuing on.

"After you *allegedly* overheard the commander, then what?"

Augie shrugs. "I was young, naive. Still had the audacity to think we were there to help folks out."

"So you..."

"Blew the whistle. Well, eventually. I can tell you I thought long and hard on it that night. Longest night of my life. I was young and stupid but not so stupid as to realize what I learned wasn't small potatoes. I knew whatever I did next was going to have serious consequences and I was pissed about that. I didn't ask for this knowledge. I just wanted to survive the war, get home, meet girls and go to ball games."

"And?"

"Like I said, I blew the whistle and then, as the young people like to say today, life kind of went to shit. Privates aren't suppose to make accusations like that against brass."

"So what happened?"

"To the Commander? Best of my knowledge, nothing.

Scot free."

"And you?"

"After I made my first accusations I was, let's see, what would be the appropriate word... sequestered. I was shipped to the closest American base, pronto, and grilled by I can't begin to tell you how many people. They assured me it wasn't true. That I'd misheard the conversation."

"Were you scared?"

"Hell yes! Nearly crapped my pants! You try being locked in a room and interrogated by men who've got the power to pretty much do with me as they saw fit. You bet I was plenty scared. And they made their point abundantly clear."

"Which was?"

"I keep my yap shut. The thought of life in Leavenworth can be very persuasive to a young man." Augie pauses for a moment to sip his coffee. "But what really chapped my ass were the constant calls for years after."

"Calls?"

"Threats, really. Reminders that if I revisited the subject with anyone there would be...consequences. Last one came about ten months ago. It's like the call is permanently scheduled. Every year, like clockwork. But what bugs me the most about it is the goddamn attitude."

"Intimidating? Threatening?"

"Oh, it's threatening all right. There's no mistaking their intent. It's just that the call is always so formal and polite. I dunno...so professional. Like they're reminding me not to forget my dentist appointment the next day. Almost like they're reading off a script. It's always the same..."*Hello, Mr. Perlman. This is just a reminder of our agreement. Thank you for taking the time to consider your commitment to the matter at hand. If we learn that you have not lived up to our agreement one of our representatives will visit you at a time of our convenience. Thank you for your consideration.*'"

"Damn."

"No kidding. The line that always gave me the creeps was the one about visiting me at a time of their convenience. Shorthand for I'd never see them coming."

"So why tell your story now?"

Augie waves a hand dismissively. "I'm an old man. Tired of playing by their rules. Screw 'em."

"Do you ever regret what you did?"

"I don't know if you've figured it out yet, but around these parts loyalty is the coin of the realm. That's the way I was raised."

"But..."

"I couldn't live with myself knowing what the old man was doing. I even learned that they tattooed the women, to keep track of their product. Subtle marks that they could pass off as birthmarks. Can you imagine?"

"How do you think the other residents of Little Norway will feel when they find out you ratted out your superior officer? Even though it was seventy years ago."

"Don't care. Carrying around secrets is a heavy burden and I'm too old to carry this one around anymore." The old woman from the kitchen brings in an old ceramic coffee pot and starts refilling their cups. Web stares at his notes and shakes his head.

"It's an amazing story, but how can you prove it?"

Augie produces a small, ancient, beat up leather book, and sets it on the TV tray. "I kept a journal. Figured one day it might come in handy."

Web delicately picks up the journal and gives it a skeptical glance. "I'm no lawyer but..."

"I also have Chloe."

"Who's Chloe?"

"My wife."

Web looks up at the quiet woman pouring coffee.

"What can she prove?"

Chloe responds by setting down the coffee pot and pulling her long, gray hair over to reveal a faded, ragged mark inked into the back of her neck.

26

Web enters Grace's market looking over his notes in his notebook. He shakes his head in wonder. Could Augie's story possibly be true? Grace is behind the counter, leaning over; elbows propped on the countertop; she's flipping through a magazine.

"Hey, Grace, what's up?

Grace looks up from her gossip rag. "George Clooney is still single. I've still got a chance."

Web smiles. "You'd eat him alive."

Grace doesn't miss a beat. "And he would be delicious."

Web pulls out an envelope, already stamped and ready for mailing. He casually drops it on the counter. He does a quick about face and heads over to the magazine rack.

Grace comes out from behind the counter, strides over and stops in front of Web. He looks up to see her staring intently at him. He glances around, wondering if he's missing something. "Uh, Grace, something you want?"

She stands there, hands on hips, head cocked at an angle, her foot tapping out a staccato beat, the picture of an impatient woman. "Is there something you wanted to tell me?"

Web looks puzzled. His eyes flash back and forth again.

143

He answers slowly, unsurely. "Don't think so."

Grace looks skeptical. "Nothing. Nothing at all." She slowly withdraws an envelope from her apron pocket and dangles it in front of his face. "So you're saying you just plain forgot to tell me that you already sent out a letter to a publisher?"

Web's eyes light up and he snatches the letter from her hand. While he's clumsily trying to open it he casts her a sheepish look. "Four actually. I sent query letters to four publishers. Sent them from Pa's house. Didn't want anyone to know yet."

Grace hits him playfully with her dust rag. "Well, thanks for keeping us in the loop, you miserable bastard. So, c'mon, I'm an old woman, I haven't got all day."

Web finally rips the envelope open and does a quick scan of the letter. It only takes a second to see what the response is. Web visibly deflates.

Graces rests a sympathetic hand on his shoulder. "Sorry, hon, their loss."

Web regains his composure and slaps a confident smile back on his face. "Hey, not the first one of these I've gotten. There's still three more letters out there, right?"

"Damn straight." Grace turns and heads back over to the counter. Once her back is turned Web looks grimly back down at the rejection letter. He takes a deep breath and slowly folds up the letter and places it inside his notebook. With his head still down he fires off a question at Grace, a smile in his voice, but it's the kind of smile you hear when you ask someone how they are and they say "Doing great!" when you know damn well they aren't.

In other words, he's not fooling anyone. "So Grace, what was the Allies password on D-Day?"

Grace answers without even looking up. "Mickey Mouse."

Despite the rejection letter's bruise to his ego, Web smiles, and for the umpteenth time shakes his head in amazement at Grace's encyclopedic knowledge. He turns his attention back to the magazine rack.

While he's perusing the rack Grace picks up the letter that Web dropped on the counter. It's addressed to Nicholas Weller. Grace silently opens a drawer and puts the letter in the outgoing mail tray. The incoming mail tray has a couple of returned letters from Web to his father, unopened, stamped "Return to Sender." She turns them over, face down, and closes the drawer.

Web, down on his haunches, checking the lowest row of the magazine rack hollers over his shoulder. "Has my latest writing magazine shown up?"

"Shoot, I completely forgot." Grace takes a magazine from behind the counter and walks it over to Web. "Just in."

He leaps up and meets her half way to take it. "Thanks." Web eagerly flips through the magazine before stopping short. He stares down at the page. The glossy, full-page photo of Sal Shelby stares back. Sal is dressed immaculately in chinos, a starched, open-neck white dress shirt and forest green blazer. He looks extremely authorish. Web half expects to see a pipe in one hand. The article's title in bold, masculine type: "*Shelby Races to front of Literary Pack.*" A weak tie to the sports car of the same name. Web can practically see the smirking editor giggling at his own cleverness. Asshole.

Web flips the page, and again. There's a photo of Sal at some high-end gala event, his arm casually draped over the shoulder of Charlize Theron. Another of him mugging with Johnny Depp. Web's teeth begin to grind. The article stops three pages in with the helpful instruction that the article continues on page 93.

Grace notices the change in Web's composure. "Anything wrong?"

Web slaps the magazine close and gathers himself. "I'm fine. Hey, Grace, mind if I use your computer again?"

"Sure. Holly's in back using it right now, but you can jump on right after her. I thought you were getting a laptop."

"I am. I will. Still looking."

Grace leads Web into the back. The room's partially torn up, plastic hanging on the walls, new drywall still unmudded. "Again, sorry about the mess. Still got a ways to go. If nobody's ever told you, dry rot is a pain in the ass." Holly is sitting at the surprisingly new looking computer, typing away.

"Help yourself right after Holly's done," Grace says. "If you're surfing for porn sites just make sure you write them down so I can find them again." She smiles, gives Web a reassuring pat on the shoulder and leaves him to it. She gives one last disgusted look around the wreck of a room and shakes her head. "I sometimes wonder if I'll ever get this place back together again. I almost actually feel a smidge guilty about Pa keeping so much of my stuff."

Grace begins picking up, and doing some minor tidying.

Web wanders over to the computer and glances over Holly's shoulder. He can't help but crack wise. "What you working on? Ballistic variances? Weaponology?" Holly responds with a look teenagers give their idiotic parents. Web ignores it with a smile. "Seriously, what are you doing?"

Holly gives him a long stare and comes to the conclusion that he's serious. "I'm writing a story too."

"Really? About what?"

She does another long check of his sincerity. Satisfied, she owns up. "It's the story of a small town girl making her first trip to the big city. I swear, you laugh I'll belt you!"

Web throws up his hands in defense. "Who's laughing? I think it's great you're writing."

"You do?"

"Sure. Hell, maybe you'll get published before me."

"How does someone get published, anyhow?"

Web's a bit surprised by her legitimate and earnest question. He pulls up a chair beside her. "Well, first you write a query letter to a publisher giving a brief description of your book or article. Hold on." Web digs through his astoundingly disorganized folder and miraculously finds what he's looking for. "Like this." Web hands her a letter.

"This is one of my queries."

Web's brain dials back to the first query letter he sent to a publisher. It was for an unsolicited article on sniper rifles (hey, you write what you know) to a high-end gun enthusiast magazine. He couldn't believe they didn't bite. How could they possibly turn down an article about sniper rifles written by an actual sniper? At the time he was so pissed he couldn't see straight. Of course hindsight being what it is he probably would have thrown the query in the trash as well. He was still no expert but looking back it was a pretty dreadful attempt: incorrectly formatted, wrong font, single spaced, and worst of all it didn't sell the concept. Amateurish at best. He considered resending a new and improved query but knew if the publisher recognized his name or the article pitch it would be tossed virtually on principle.

Holly looks over the query Web handed her. "So what if the publisher likes the idea?"

"Then they send you a letter asking for a proposal."

"What's a proposal?"

"Hoo-boy. Let's see. A proposal is, well, it's more detail, more information about the story and why the publisher should consider taking you on. Maybe you've got lots of people who read your blog, or maybe you're on TV, or maybe your dad is Bill Gates. Publishers are always looking for an author who has an added edge."

Holly thinks on that for a moment. "What's your added edge?"

Web purses his lips in thought. "Good question. Still figuring that out."

"So you don't have one."

Web stares at the girl. What is it with teenagers and their freakin' condescending, bullshit attitudes? You just want to smack 'em. The thing that pisses him off though, what really rubs him raw, is she's right; he doesn't have one. At least one he's willing to use.

Holly continues with her questioning. "And if they like the proposal?"

Web had been thoroughly enjoying the back and forth, at least until her last crack, and tries to steer the ship back on course. "Then they send a letter asking for a manuscript." Web knows what she's about to ask so he jumps right in, beats her to the punch. It's become a flirty game. "And if they like the manuscript...then you get published."

Web is clearly enjoying being in a position of knowledge and Holly seems sincerely interested. "Have you ever gotten a letter from a publisher saying they liked one of your ideas?"

Web casts a furtive glance at Grace who gives him a reassuring nod before he turns back to Holly. "Uh, no." He can see this last admission of failure pretty much shuts down any interest she previously had. He scrambles to recover. "Luckily, people's tastes are subjective. If one publisher doesn't like something, another might love it. There were all sorts of publishers who turned down Harry Potter."

"Seriously?"

"Yep." Her interest is still wavering so he takes another tack. "You ever heard of a writer named Sal Shelby?" She shakes her head no. Web actually feels a stab of satisfaction. He pulls out the magazine with the article on Sal, opens it to the page and hands it over to her. "Sal's the guy in the blue suit. See who he's standing next to?"

"Oh my God! Is that Johnny Depp?"

"Yep. See, Sal's a friend of mine. We served together.

Good man. Good soldier. You'd like him." Web leans back and speaks in Grace's direction. "You'd like him too, Grace. He's a big antique gun collector."

Grace hollers back, "I like him already. Is he hot looking?"

Web glances at Holly, who nods enthusiastically. "Uh...Holly says yes."

"Good enough for me," says Grace and continues with her puttering.

Web turns his attention back to Holly. "I suppose if I was really hard up I could always tap into Sal's connections."

"What publisher is Sal with?"

"Brentwood Publishing." It takes a beat for Web to realize he's disappointed he was able to call the name up so quickly and effortlessly.

Holly looks excited. "See, you do have an edge!" But her look of excitement quickly changes to puzzlement. "But I don't get it. If you've got an inside connection with a publisher how come you still haven't gotten anything published?"

Web takes a cleansing breath. "I'll tell you the same thing I told Sal: Because I want to get published on my own talent, without outside help."

Holly considers that for a second. "That seems kind of stupid. Why not get your foot in the door first then get all holier-than-thou after you're rich enough to tell people to screw off? I mean, what happens if nobody bites on your war stories book? What are you gonna do then?"

Goddam teenagers.

Web gives her a confident nod. "I always say you're only as good as your Plan-B."

"So what's your Plan-B?"

Web chews on that for a second. "I've got some ideas." And leaves it at that.

At that moment Holly checks her watch and jumps up. "Shoot, I gotta go. The computer's yours." She makes sure that before she leaves she reaches over to pick up her notes, letting her hair drift over Web's face. She gives him another look and slips away.

Grace, oblivious to the interaction, finishes her tidying and grabs Holly as she passes.

"Hold it, young lady. You can give me a hand with some boxes out front before you skedaddle." The two women leave the room.

Alone, Web regroups, looks over his notes and stares down the keyboard. The keyboard: the Rubik's cube for writers. Figure out the puzzle, the correct sequence of keystrokes, tap them in a particular order and the world opens up for you like Pharaoh's Tomb. Type them in the wrong sequence and pffft, nothing. There are 26 letters in the alphabet, billions of word combinations. Web would give his right nut to know that right sequence of keystrokes. They say if you put a million monkeys in front of a million typewriters, odds are one of them will end up typing War and Peace. Web thinks whoever came up with that mathematical analogy can kiss his ass.

Web sits back in his chair, thinking for a moment before leaning forward and making a few stabs at the traitorous keyboard. He calls up the Google search engine.

In the search window he types in Sal Shelby's name. In a split second he sees there are over 500,000 web pages dedicated to Sal the author. Web sits back again, pauses, then, what the hell, he Googles himself. Zero web pages. Bupkis. Quietly, to himself, he wonders aloud, "So what's your Plan-B, Web?" He slumps down, looking forlornly at his notebook. Suddenly the idea springs on him. The one action that's always been his emotional cure-all. In fact, it's what brought him to Little Norway in the first place. The words spontaneously pop out of his mouth, "Road trip."

Road trip. The phrase made famous in National Lampoon's 1978 comedy *Animal House*. After Dean Wormer, played pitch-perfectly by notorious heavy John Vernon, shuts down the Delta House fraternity and confiscates everything (Even the stuff we didn't steal!), Otter and Boon, to forget their troubles, utter the immortal words, "Road trip." Ever since Web saw that movie—the first time a sanitized, bleeped-out version on TBS—he became a fervent disciple of the healing power of road trips. His first one, sophomore year at Shorecrest high school, home of the kilt-clad Highlanders, he and his two best friends Erik Kaye and Scotty "Dawg" Allen split for the coast in an effort to salve Web's bruised ego from being dumped by Leslie Farmington. They'd been dating for over a month so in Web's 16-year-old eyes that constituted official girlfriendishness. Granted, he'd never gone all the way with her, actually never made it past second base, but there was always that hope on the horizon. But with one simple sentence (It's not you, it's me) six weeks of dating equity got unceremoniously flushed down the shitter. Three Pabst Blue Ribbons later, kiped from his dad's cooler, he and his *boyz* were on the road, blasting 4 Non Blondes, Green Day and Aerosmith, cursing the puzzle that is women and bonding the way only teenage boys can over the course of a three hour drive to the coast. From that day on road trips became the duct tape in his emotional toolbox. The all purpose fix-it for life's troubles.

Web starts digging into his backpack. "Get away for a day, clear my head." He takes out the Minnesota tour book that he found in Pa's storage room. "So what spectacular international tourist attractions might I find near beautiful Little Norway?" He opens the book and the train ticket he inadvertently slipped inside back at Pa's house falls out on to the table. He sets it aside without a thought and starts paging through the book, but after a beat he stops and looks back at the faded ticket. His eyes come to rest on the date: November 21st, 1963. Something about the date. A thought comes to him. He Googles the date. The computer screen fills with options, none promising. He clicks on the first one. "Nicolette Sheridan's birthday. Hmm, don't see Pa being a big *Desperate Housewives* fan." He tries again with a slightly different date. "November 20th". Still nothing of consequence. One more try. "November 22nd, 1963." He hits the return button and instantaneously the screen has Web's full attention.

"Holy crap."

He glances at the door again to make sure Grace isn't coming before turning back to the computer screen.

153

He fishes out his note pad and pen and begins taking furious notes. Again, quietly to himself, "Plan-B. Plan-B." After surfing the web for a while and quickly filling up his notebook he checks his watch. "Shit." He hastily throws his stuff together, returns the browser to Grace's home page and bolts. Leaving the back room and cutting through the market, he passes Grace at the counter. "Thanks, Grace."

"Where you heading off to in such a hurry?"

"I'm late for an interview. See ya."

As he rushes out the door, Grace calls out after him, "Did you remember to shut down the computer?" but it's evident he doesn't hear her. Grace shakes her head. "Kids. I swear." She walks into the back room. Sure enough, he left the computer on. "That's it, just suck out all my electricity. Sure, go ahead, money grows on trees." She's about to turn it off but pauses. She sits down and stares thoughtfully at the screen. She grabs the mouse and navigates the cursor into the computer's web history. She clicks, again and again. What pops up on the screen is page after page dedicated to the assassination of President John F Kennedy.

27

Web is at Bart Tinker's house. Bart was the Veteran's Day MC at the Cabin, the man with the cane, which he is currently resting across his lap. Up close Web can see it's not standard hospital issue. No gray metal tube with the requisite foam padded question mark handle, this cane is a work of art. A dark wood stick, maybe stained hickory, topped with a scalloped brass transition to a carved L-shaped ivory handle. Web wonders if there's a two-foot steel pig-sticker hidden in the shaft.

Their interview finished, Web pockets his tape recorder and raises from his chair. With the help of his cane Bart slowly gets to his feet as well and shows Web to the door. At the door Web turns to shake his hand. "Thank you very much for sharing your stories, Mr. Tinker."

"From now on it's just Bart, and my pleasure."

"Quite frankly I'm a bit surprised at the reaction I've gotten. Seems like most everyone is willing to talk about their military past. Well, some less than others."

"That'd be Pa you're referring to."

"That'd be him."

"No surprise there. There are two things he *don't like* to talk about: his family and his past. And one thing you *don't want him* to talk about: politics."

"I kind of learned that last one the hard way. I made some comment about President Kennedy and Viet Nam..."

"Oh, boy."

"Just about bit my head off."

"Yes, young Jack of Camelot was never very popular with Pa. Something about him that just rubbed Pa the wrong way."

"Huh, go figure. Well, thanks again for your time." Web steps out the door, gets a few feet away, stops and turns to face Bart. "Just out of curiosity, how did Pa's wife die anyway?"

The old man's face slowly falls. "It was a sorry, sordid mess. Like I said, not a subject you'd want to bring up with Pa. Or Grace for that matter. But I figure you ought to know what makes Pa tick, seeing as you're living under the same roof." Bart limps down the steps and takes a seat on the lowest. "They hadn't been married long before Helen's desire for life in the big city finally got the better of her, and she actually convinced Pa they should move to Washington D.C." Bart stops to recollect. "Now Pa would've walked on water for that girl, so off they went. Then little Jacob was born. This was also about the time that Pa was being deployed a lot. He'd be gone for months at a time on some top-secret mission or another. I guess it's no surprise that with the challenges of a new baby and an absentee husband Helen finally started looking for adult companionship elsewhere." Bart begins doodling in the dirt with the tip of his cane, keeping his eyes down. "Rumor has it that she hooked up with some serious DC bigwig. Broke poor Pa's heart. When he found out she was having an affair he packed his bags, took the boy and was back here in Little Norway, lickity-split." Bart looks back up to Web. "About a week later Helen calls him up, falling all over herself apologizing, begging for him to take her back. Said there was a good reason for what she did. Said she had something important to tell him."

"And?"

"She never got the chance. A week later she was found dead in a shady DC park. Mugging, they figured. Pa was inconsolable. Grace, maybe even worse."

"A mugging?"

"Pa didn't like the answer either. Was convinced there was something more. Spent all of his spare time making trips back and forth to DC trying to dig up answers. You'd think with Pa's military connections and his black bag experience he would have found something if there was anything shady to be found. That's what Pa did back in the day. He tracked things down. Weren't no one better from what I hear."

"What did he find?"

"To the best of my knowledge? Nothing. Poor Pa, loses a wife, and then later, his son. He's been through more pain than ten men put together."

Web thanks the man for his time and walks up the street. His mind now Dolores Packed with more questions than answers.

28

Later that night, Web sits on the edge of his bed staring down at pages and pages spread out all over the bed. He picks a random page and quietly summarizes. "The Bataan Death March." He picks up another page. "The Chosin Reservoir." Another page. A longer pause. "Augie Perlman." While Web shakes his head in amazement he starts collecting the papers into a pile and slips them back inside his notebook. Right then there's a soft knock at his door. Pa peers in.

"You've been in here all evening. Can I get you a cup of coffee or something?"

"No thanks, I'm good."

"I understand you heard back from a publisher already. Sorry the response wasn't what you wanted."

"Thanks, Pa. It's frustrating. Sometimes I think I just don't understand what it is they want."

"Judging by what I see on the newsstands, anything cheap, sleazy or sensational. Afraid there's a short supply of that 'round these parts. Well, good night." Pa slips out the door, closing it softly behind him.

Web stares down at the notebook in his hand. Across the cover written in thick black pen on a piece of masking tape is his book's working title, "A Town of Heroes". He reflects on the title. "Not exactly cheap, sleazy, or..." Web stops in thought. "Sensational." Web goes to the door, listens at it for a moment and then turns and quietly reaches down to take a manila folder out from under his mattress. He sits on the far side of the bed with his back turned to the door. He takes out the pages. They're his notes on the Kennedy assassination. Web looks them over a moment, finally shakes his head and puts the papers back. "Keep your eye on the ball, Weller." He carefully places the manila folder back under his mattress and makes sure everything looks as it should.

There's another soft knock at the door and Pa peers back in holding a phone, one hand cupped over the receiver. "Sorry to bother you again but Rose Fulkerson wants to know if you'd like apple crisp or marionberry pie for your interview with her."

Web glances at his watch. "Crap, I'm late."

Pa affords him a smile. "I'd recommend the apple crisp."

Web grabs his notebook and bolts past Pa. "No rest for the wicked."

As Pa watches him head out the front door, "And the good don't need it."

29

The following days are a blur of activity for Web.
Between interviews, transcribing the conversations and
doing research virtually every waking hour is accounted
for. He's been spending so much time sitting down he's
actually formed the early stages of a good old fashioned
spare tire. Well, maybe a bike inner tube. Web wonders if
this is what it's like, the life of a writer: activity without
a lick of exercise. A few months ago Web wouldn't have
thought that was possible. For the past decade his life has
been dedicated to honing his body and mind to a razor's
edge. The writing and research have kept him mentally
sharp but it's a totally different discipline. During his years
in the military all his brainpower was directed to strategy,
tactics and trying to outthink the target. It was a decade-
long chess match with a revolving series of opponents.
And it could be exhausting. When you're hiding in a blind
or lying perfectly still in a ghillie suit, blending into a
background, waiting hours on end for your target to reveal
him or herself the stress level isn't bad. You are alert but
relaxed. Of course the anxiety level is proportional to your
threat level. If you aren't worried about being discovered
by kids, dogs, farmers or some random guy looking for
a place to piss then the stress level is low. But when a

target appears or you get the aforementioned flies-in-the-ointment then the blood starts pumping. There's a reason the First Marine Division Scout Sniper School's motto is *Suffer Patiently* and *Patiently Suffer*. When you're in enemy territory it's hard work keeping your adrenaline in check knowing that one false move can put you square in the cross-hairs of someone who, like yourself, is collecting a military paycheck to kill people on the other side. You being that guy on the other side. You heard stories about soldiers in Viet Nam, about how focused they'd be when running point on a patrol. Wading through thick jungle, every one of their senses cranked up to a frequency only dogs can hear, desperately hoping they're not hovering in a sniper's iron sights, ready to be dropped and forgotten with three pounds of pull on a trigger. A soldier running point could lose five pounds of stress-related weight in a couple of hours without doing anything more physical than walking. Being "on" is the greatest diet known to man, if you don't die from the stress.

Another factor to his recent weight gain: cookies. Non-stop. At every interview he's constantly treated to a vast array of cookies, brownies, muffins and coffee. Lots of coffee. Norwegian circulatory systems must run on the stuff. He thought he'd drank his share in the service but it was nothing compared to what these people could put away. The U.S. military coffee consumption didn't amount to diddly-dick in Little Norway.

One more side effect to Web's interviews: human connection. Unlike anything Web has experienced in his life. Day in, day out, Web is hip deep in shared emotion, a life experience communion of sorts. He laughs and jokes with his adopted town folk; gives a shoulder to cry on and listens. Always listens. Perhaps that's become his greatest gift to the people of Little Norway; he listens to them. That was another thing pounded into him by his mother. "People don't like talkers as much as they like listeners," she'd say. Another was, "Better to keep your mouth shut and be thought a fool than to open it and remove all doubt." These words of wisdom had served Web well since he'd been in Little Norway, with its disproportionate number of vets and disproportionate number of elderly. One of the great fears of old age is the fear of becoming irrelevant, outdated, inconsequential. Like a computer that's become obsolete and ignored in favor of a newer model. It is a fear that becomes harsh reality through subtle actions over years. You're the head of a family, or perhaps a business; people look up to you, value your opinion. But the kids move away, retirement removes you from your position of power, and before you know it no one seems that interested in what you have to say anymore. You've become the classic grumpy old man or crotchety old woman because *Kids these days, they got no respect for their elders.*

But Web listens. And those he listens to are relevant once again even if only for the time it takes them to recall their stories of service between nibbled bites of shortbread and a pot of Folgers (Mountain grown!).

But the emotions are not all good. Another query letter goes out for his Town of Heroes book; another rejection letter comes in while Web gamely smiles through gritted teeth. The weight of his JFK research, more a curiosity, a second tier project behind the book, grows heavier by the day. Covertly slipping the manila envelope back under his mattress is becoming a daily ritual. Before long a third rejection letter arrives.

Web knows rejection letters are standard operating procedure in the writing game but it doesn't make it any easier. It still sucks having someone tell you they don't think your skills are up to snuff. He decides to clear his mind and take a leisurely stroll through town.

Leaving Pa's house, he heads down the road toward Grace's market but breaks off on one of the handful of streets that make up Little Norway and heads north in the general direction of the Cabin. It's a Wednesday, pretty quiet, most folks either at work or holed up inside, watching game shows or surfing the Internet. He passes Ruth Woolworth's house. Tough to miss. You can usually hear it before you see it. Ruthie runs the only daycare service in town so there's always the high pitched squeal of ankle-biters emanating from her hurricane-fenced yard. Small children have always been a complete mystery to Web. He doesn't doubt that when the time comes he'll be a good father, at least that's what he tells himself, but in the meantime the motivations and thought processes of little kids are as foreign and puzzling to him as high math.

Web wanders by Ruthie's yard and glances in at the daily destruction. The beaten grass rectangle is an elephant's graveyard of discarded toys and dilapidated playground equipment. Web figures it's safe to say the place wouldn't pass a half-blind insurance adjuster's inspection. An empty tire-swing hangs morosely from an ancient white oak that's currently in full, spectacular broad-leafed form. The swing's tattered rope doesn't look like it could hold more weight than a sack of flour. Maybe the kids have some sort of preternatural ability to sense that the swing is an accident waiting to happen, but Web doubts it. If these kids act anything like he did as a tyke they would have absolutely no clue as to what is safe and what is dangerous. That might explain Web's numerous trips to the emergency room growing up. It's generous to say that small children simply don't know better but it's probably more accurate to say they're just kind of stupid. *Hey, I bet we can make a parachute out of this tablecloth and jump from the roof! I know, let's play hockey in the basement with golf clubs!* For the record, bad ideas, both.

There are four kids currently wreaking high-pitched havoc while Ruthie watches over them with a warm smile and a cigarette burning lazily, hanging from the corner of her mouth. She and Web trade congenial waves.

Two of the kids, a boy and a girl, are in the sandbox conjuring up imaginary architecture with shovels and pails. The boy is Dexter and Mary Pace's kid, the girl belongs to Penny Sullivan, at least Monday through Friday and every other weekend. Web's never met the dad but word on the street is he's a third generation boozer who raised one too many hands to Penny in a drunken rage and came out on the expected short end of the soon-to-follow divorce and custody proceedings.

One little boy is riding around on a tricycle like the

devil himself was hot at his heels. The boy is wearing a threadbare Yankees baseball cap that is barely hanging on as the child purposefully spins out the trike in the area at the far end of the yard where the grass has given up the ghost. The kid backs up the trike and powers in for a second spin out, then a third. A thick cloud of dust has risen up from his efforts causing Ruthie to holler good-naturedly at him to settle down. The boy answers with a gap-toothed smile and a fourth spin out for good measure.

The last child is a tow-headed girl in a shabby pale blue dress that's probably been worn by four girls before her. On her head perches a well-worn pair of Mickey Mouse ears. The girl sits quietly by the oak rocking back and forth and twiddling her fingers together in a non-stop rhythm, like she's playing an overly complex piece of music on a piano but with her opposing fingers taking the place of the keys. She's staring down at the grass like there's something of ultimate fascination hiding in the blades but Web can't see what it might be. He suspects it's nothing. The little girl's name is Marcie and she's the daughter of Mike and Leslie Bishop, a sweetheart of a couple who live next door to Augie Perlman. From what Augie says Marcie has been diagnosed with something called Asperger's syndrome. It's on the low end of the Autism spectrum. Like the little girl marches to a drummer that only she hears. She has a hell of a time making friends because her social skills aren't nearly in the ballpark of normal. Poor Mike and Leslie were pulling their hair out trying to find something that Marcie could engage in and lo and behold that something took the shape of the Wonderful World of Disney. For whatever reason little Marcie lights up like a pinball machine when anything Disney related is before her. Tinkerbell, Mickey, one of the Princesses, doesn't matter. As a result Marcie has become the resident expert on all things developed and marketed by the Walt Disney Corporation and her bedroom has become an absolute shrine to the House of Mouse.

Augie told Web that a TV station in Minneapolis got word of her over-the-top Disney-themed bedroom and sent a crew up to do a story on the small town Asperger's girl with the Disney fetish. To top it off, last year everyone in town pitched in and bought Marcie and her parents a week's vacation in Disneyland. Roundtrip flight for the whole family, hotel, meals, the works. Word has it that little Marcie got more smileage out of those seven days than the rest of her life combined. Happiest place on earth indeed.

As these thoughts cross Web's mind it dawns on him that he's becoming more and more Little Norway-ized by the day. He's getting to know the families, their backgrounds and even a few secrets. He knows the gossip and dirt as well as any housewife sharing stories across backyard fences. He's been thoroughly dipped in small town culture and darned if it doesn't appeal to him.

Web reaches the end of Ruthie's fence and looks ahead. At the end of the block and catty-corner is Little Norway's cemetery. A low black wrought iron fence surrounds the one block square. A gap in the fence serves as an entrance; there is no gate. Web figures what would be the purpose?

He steps inside and looks the grounds over. Arlington Memorial in Virginia could not be tidier and better kept. The grass has been freshly cut to a fairway's length and to Web's eyes there's nary a weed in sight. Virtually every tombstone and grave marker holds flowers or small flags, remnants of Memorial Day.

Web thinks back to when he was a kid and he and his buddies would ride their bikes through the nearby cemetery. The wide, winding paths and lack of traffic made an irresistible location. They also had a game where they would see who could find the oldest grave. The best Web ever found was some guy who'd kicked it in 1935, which to a boy in the early 1990's was an impossibly long time ago. The man had the unforgettable name of Thelonious Keiser. A name that ranks right up there with Grace's CMH recipient Smedley Darlington Butler. Web wondered if Thelonious got beat up a lot for having such a ridiculous name or if maybe Thelonious was the Mike or Steve of the day. Web also couldn't help but wonder what Thelonious Keiser was like. He'd died at the ripe old age of 82 so when he was the same age as Web when he and his pals cruised BMX's through the tombstones it had to have been somewhere around the American Civil War. Did Thelonious, still just a kid, take up arms against the Rebs? Was he given a rifle as tall as himself and told to stand a post or march into a picket line of bearded men in gray, twice or three times his age? Probably not since he came out of the back side of the war and lived another sixty-five to seventy years.

Web wanders through the immaculate gravesites,

again playing the game of find the oldest tombstone (Daphne Keene, 1884). On his way back to the entrance Web stops at one marker that has caught his eye. The headstone itself is nothing special, a small granite rectangle, dull and weathered. It's the name etched on the front that gives Web pause: Norris Hoolie. Web looks over at the identical stone just to the right. Marie Hoolie. Grace's parents no doubt. According to the headstones Marie passed in '92 at the age of ninety, while Norris left to play with the Choir Invisible only a year later, coming up just shy of a hundred. Man, wouldn't that suck. Dying at ninety-nine. Every day of that last year ol' Norrie probably woke up thinking just let me make it to a hundred, just give me a few more months. And then every time he'd feel a tickle in his heart or his left arm would get numb he'd think, shit, not yet. On his deathbed he probably wasn't scared, he was probably pissed for coming up short.

Web gives the grave of Norris Hoolie a respectful nod and walks out of the cemetery the way he came in.

30

Web starts heading back home. Pa's house technically, but Web has noticed he's begun to think of it as home. If he's considering sticking around Little Norway for any amount of time he should probably consider looking for a place of his own but in the meantime he's about as content as he's been in a coon's age and Pa seems to enjoy his company. Even Holly doesn't seem to mind having him about, but with her teenager's general air of indifference it's hard to tell.

Passing Grace's market, Web decides to drop in for a visit. Until the day he dies he doesn't think he will ever tire of chatting with the woman. When he walks in the bell hanging over the door says someone's here. A radio, somewhere in the market is tuned to a local blues station. The singer is croaking on about how someone did someone wrong and how his woman done left him. The sound is at muzak levels. Purely background.

Web spots Grace sitting behind the counter, her back to the door but her head swivels around at the sound of the bell. Even from across the room Web can see the glint of tears in her eyes. She flashes a brave smile and waves him in quickly followed by a drag across her eyes with her left sleeve.

"It's okay, Web. No one died. C'mon in."

Web has never seen Grace cry before. If possible, the mere presence of tears makes him like her even more than before. It humanizes her, softens her. Judging by the level of redness around her eyes it wasn't a full-blown gullywasher of tears, just a small leak in the dam that was quickly patched. Despite Grace's smile, the concern on Web's face hasn't dimmed appreciably, at least not enough to suit Grace. She waves him in a second time and points to one of the chairs along the wall under the Mannlicher rifle. "Really, Web, honest and for true, it's all good. Pull up a chair."

Web slides the chair over behind the counter, spins it around backwards and plops himself down with his legs straddling the chair back. "Why were you crying?"

Grace makes another dab at her eyes with the heel of her right hand and gives a small laugh. "Oh, I was just taking a stroll down memory lane. I can be such a sap at times." She reaches over to a stout cardboard box on the floor that Web hadn't noticed and slides it over between them before taking a seat in the opposing chair. She reaches inside the box, one that in a former life held bottles of Jack Daniels, and pulls out a handful of envelopes. Judging by the yellow tint of the paper they are evidently quite old. "Letters my dad wrote to my ma back when he was overseas."

Grace has never talked about her parents before. The fact that Grace knows more about the military than just about anyone Web has ever met combined with her affinity for veterans makes it a no-brainer that her father would have been a vet himself, but for whatever reason the thought has never crossed Web's mind. He feels slightly foolish at the oversight.

Grace draws out one letter in particular and looks it over longingly. "He was stationed in France during the Great War. World War I to the uninitiated." Grace pauses for a moment, her train of thought switching rails. "Do you know how World War 1 got started?"

Web nods. "An assassination." It's been over a decade since his military classes and some of the information is still rattling around in his skull, just not all collated and organized.

Grace nods. "Archduke Francis Ferdinand, heir to the Habsburg crown, basically the royalty of Austria-Hungary. He and his wife were gunned down in Sarajevo by a Serbian, a member of the terrorist group with an awesome name..." Grace holds up her hands and makes them into claws like a bad horror movie monster, "... *The Black Hand*."

Web smiles for her benefit, enjoying the history lesson.

Grace brings her hands back into her lap and tips her hed slightly, giving Web a quizzical look. "Think about that. One man is shot and as a result over a hundred thousand people die. The rule of unintended consequences played out in full form." Grace shakes her head in disgust before looking back at Web and throwing up her hands with practically a shout. "And the thing is, the Archduke? Nobody really even liked him that much. He wasn't mister popularity!"

"So why all the hubbub?"

"Well, up to that point there were two sides that were really pissed at each other. Maybe not pissed, but definitely jealous. There was one group of nations made up of Germany, Austria and Italy known as *The Triple Alliance*, and then there were the other guys, *The Triple Entente*, made up of Great Britain, France and Russia. America wasn't even in the picture. For years these two groups were just an incident away from breaking out the brass knuckles and they got it with the Ferdinand assassination. Basically it became a convenient excuse for Austria-Hungary to go after Serbia. After that it was just dominos. So-and-so declared war on so-and-so and on it went, one nation after another. It wasn't until almost three years later, 1917, when three American ships were sunk by German subs that the U.S. jumped in with both feet." At this Grace spreads her hands before her. "And the rest, as they say, is history."

"Did he see much action? Your dad?"

Grace rolls her eyes at the thought. "Oh, heavens yes."

"But he survived it." It was a statement not a question. He'd seen the man's gravestone.

"He did indeed." Grace settles back into her chair, the letter still held in her hand, now resting on her lap. A long distance glaze washes over her face as she draws from her memory. "He was a Marine. Hadn't been over there too long before he discovered their uniforms were virtually indistinguishable from the enemies."

"Yikes."

Grace nods in agreement. "Yikes is right. They had to

borrow uniforms from the Army, if you can believe that. It was that or take the chance of getting shot at by your own side."

"What happened to him?"

Grace cocks an eyebrow at him. "Ever see the movie *Paths of Glory*? Kirk Douglas?"

"I haven't."

"You should. Give you a right clear idea of how miserable and terrifying it was on the front lines with the Germans, excuse me, the Hun, as my daddy liked to call 'em, staring you down from across No Man's Land."

"Trench warfare?"

"Yep. Their own underground cities. They dug in and did a hell of a lot of waiting, which according to my dad was fine by him. Every day you sat tight was another day you were alive. Trench warfare was usually a war of attrition. The defense actually held the advantage. Being in the trenches you were pretty much immune to bullets so the Hun went after you with the bombs and the gas. Nasty stuff. When either side did mount an assault—went *over the top*, as they called it—it got ugly fast. Usually meant certain death because there was nowhere to hide in No Man's Land. You were basically running directly into opposing machine gun fire. I can't even imagine."

"I'm sure he had some stories to tell."

Grace's face falls a bit. "That he did, most not very nice. However..." Grace holds up a single finger, a point about to be made, "after all he went through over there, the event that had the greatest impact on him took place about five years after the war."

"How is that?"

"Despite what he witnessed and went through over there he became enamored with that part of the world. After the war ended and he came back home he stayed on with the military and eventually got himself assigned to the American Graves Registration Service."

Web nods grimly, aware of this very important but seldom-recognized part of the military: bringing back the bodies.

Grace opens the letter that's been in her lap and delicately flattens it out across her knee. She glances up at Web. "Get a load of this." She holds the letter before her face and begins to read. "My dearest Marie. I have to tell you about the most amazing thing. We'd been on the rivers and canals of France for several days, our barges stacked with almost a thousand caskets of our boys that have been found and collected over the past five years. With each town we passed there was no incident; we were just another string of tarp-covered barges making our way to open water. But after we'd passed through Holland and crossed over into Belgium something began to happen. Apparently word had spread as to our cargo and crowds began lining the sides of the canal. A small boat pulled up along side and we were asked if we could stop long enough at the locks to allow the people to pay tribute to our dead. Needless to say we were both shocked and humbled by this request. Soon a line of cavalry of all things met us and escorted us the final leg to the locks. Upon arrival cannons were fired in salute, bugles were played and songs were sung by children. I have never seen the likes. Every head was bare and many of the citizens knelt and wept openly in recognition of the American soldiers who had given their lives to free Belgium. This was their thank you and I for one will never forget their generosity of spirit and appreciation."

Grace lets her hand holding the letter fall to her lap again. A new rim of tears has formed at her eyes and she makes no effort to hide them from Web. She smiles and shrugs with an *It is what it is* expression. "Now if that don't return your faith in humanity I don't know what will."

Web responds with the only way he can at this moment, he swings his leg over the chair back and envelops Grace with a hug, perhaps the first hug he's offered up to another human being in Lord knows how long. All he knows is if there was ever a time when a hug trumped words this was it. For Grace's part she heartily accepts the squeeze and gives one in return. In that moment something changes between them. The bond they'd shared was already strong but at that moment it strengthened and hardened like epoxy. It crossed over to another level. They rest upon each other, enjoying the connection. A harp-heavy cryin' blues instrumental quietly plays on the radio, the perfect soundtrack for the end of the scene. In a movie script it would read—Fade to black.

31

With each passing day Web feels more and more like a tabloid reporter. The more research he does on this whole Kennedy thing, the more excited—and dirtier—he feels. He thinks back to any movie he has seen where a reporter, be it newspaper or television, has got a potentially hot story but can't run with it until he or she got the single most important piece of the puzzle: corroboration: Something or someone to strengthen or support his theories with definitive evidence. But where could he find it? He didn't expect to stumble across the figurative smoking gun, the incontrovertible piece of evidence that thousands of investigators and conspiracy theorists have been searching for like the Holy Grail. No, he needed more information, better information. Information from someone in the know. An expert. But where does one find an expert on historical deaths? Particularly mysterious, sensational historical deaths?

Evidently 150 miles due east.

32

The College of St. Scholastica, home of the Saints, is a small picture postcard campus nestled in the rolling hills of Duluth, Minnesota. A low forest of deciduous trees that in the fall would put New England foliage to shame surrounds the college. The epicenter of this cradle of liberal arts is Tower Hall. Built in fits and starts between 1909-1928, quarried from "blue trap" rock and looking for all the world like a regal pale gray English castle, it would seem more fitting to see lords and ladies in high stiff collars and perfect posture strolling past its imposing walls instead of young men and women in tee shirts, baggy shorts and flip flops.

Tower Hall houses classes, faculty and administrative office, not to mention the student union hang out (Storm's Den—named after the school's St. Bernard mascot) and all-important coffee shop (The Java Express—where you can still get a tall organic fair trade peace coffee for only a buck-fiddy). The Tower is also home to the School of Arts and Letters where students learn the finer points of what the Greeks would consider the pillars of society: art, communication, languages, literature, music, philosophy, theater, theology and history. In other words there isn't a business major within spitting distance.

It is here where Web finds himself standing, comparing information on a piece of paper with what he's seeing on office doors. He wanders past underclassmen, bent with egregiously over-stuffed backpacks and clutching ubiquitous cups of coffee. *What is it with these people and coffee?*

Web finally finds what he is searching for. A knock at the door prompts a welcome from within and he steps inside the office. A large, cluttered dark wood desk squats in front of the double-hung back wall window. Behind it a small, wiry man rises from his chair to greet him with a strong handshake. "Mr. Weller, welcome to St. Scholastica, glad you could make it." His accent is subtle but decidedly Scandinavian. The man motions to a chair in front of the desk. "Have a seat."

Web sits down and begins taking out his notebook and tape recorder. "Thanks for seeing me, Professor Aronson."

"My pleasure."

"I hear an accent. Let me guess, Norwegian?"

"Swedish, actually. Came with my family in 1948, not long after the war. Couldn't speak a word of English."

"Well your English is perfect now."

"Thank you. Like many immigrants at that time I was bent on becoming as American as possible, but I just can't seem to shake my accent. Every time I think I have it beaten into submission I travel back to the homeland and resurrect it. Two steps forward, one step back." The Professor holds his hands up in the universal sign for *what are you gonna do?* After a beat he brings his hands down and lays them flat on the deep green writing blotter on his desk. "What can I do for you?"

"I'm hoping you can help me with some research. I've done a fair amount online but I think there's no substitute for a face to face interview with an expert."

The Professor smiles. "I'm flattered that you consider me an expert and I hope I can offer some insight. First, may I ask what you're doing the research for?"

"A potential article, or maybe a book. I'm a writer and recently have become fascinated with the Kennedy assassination."

The Professor chuckles. "Get in line. There has never been a shortage of literature churned out on that topic." Professor Aronson sees this comment dampens his visitor's enthusiasm and quickly holds up an arthritic finger. "But don't let that stop you. A new voice and fresh perspective are always welcome."

"I understand you actually teach a class on the subject."

"Indeed, it's part of a class I hold on critical thinking and writing. We spend the second quarter looking at the facts and evidence, go over the Warren Report and discuss the numerous conspiracy theories."

"So it sounds like you know your stuff."

"Some stuff more than others. My favorites are the little nown facts. Handy for trivia nights, cocktail parties and impressing students. For instance, did you know that the limousine that Kennedy was assassinated in remained in service until 1977?

"I had no idea."

"Or that if you had bought that particular model right off the showroom floor it would have cost you a whopping $7,347. But the presidential customizing supposedly cost an additional $200,000 in taxpayer money. They actually cut the car in half, tacked on an extra three and a half feet in length. They added all sorts of odds and ends, though virtually none in the way of security or protection. Its code name was X-100."

"The car had a code name?"

The professor seems surprised that Web would even question that. "Indeed. What fun is it to be in the government or the military if you can't give things code names?"

Web doesn't have an answer for that. He knows it's true. Some of the code names he'd seen for targets and missions sounded like they were written by dime store novelists. *Operation: Viper Bite! Code Name: Black Ice!*

Web steers the professor back to why he came to see him in the first place. "Professor, how about if we start with the most important question...do you think Lee Harvey Oswald shot John F Kennedy?"

The Professor leans back in his chair, his hands coming to rest below his sunken chest, his fingers intertwining. Web always had the movie version of a college professor lodged in his head: the tweed jacket with patches on the elbows, the clipped, formal speech, the unruly mop of hair, the subtle, red-veined cheeks and nose courtesy of the bottle of scotch hidden in the lower left hand drawer. Professor Aronson doesn't quite fit the bill. Not by a sight. He's a small man. Drawn wet from a well he still wouldn't crack a buck and a half on a scale. He is dressed in a s harply pressed blue button down dress shirt, open at the collar with a black tee shirt peeking up at the neck. Frankly, quite stylish and a younger look than his advanced age would normally recommend. His hair is pure white and cropped close. His smiling hazel eyes sit behind narrow, rimless glasses and below what can only be described as the professor's most striking features—his eyebrows: two, thick, dark, bushy shrubs that look like they were teased with a brush and colored with a Sharpie. Web can't shake the image of two black box cars slipping downhill toward each other in a subtle V, like they're destined for imminent collision. And these brows grab your attention like nobody's business.

"Mr. Weller, let us jump, as they say, into the Way Back machine and lay out the nuts and bolts of the subject at hand. President John Fitzgerald Kennedy was shot and killed on Friday, November 22nd, 1963 in the presidential limousine in Dealey Plaza, Dallas, Texas at 12:30pm. He and Jackie in the backseat, Texas governor John Connolly and his wife in the front seat. Witnesses heard three gunshots. Two bullets struck the president. The first went through his neck and then proceeded to hit governor Connolly, the second, the kill shot, struck the president in the back right portion of his head. I'm sure you've seen the home movie footage, shot by Abraham Zapruder."

"Certainly."

"Probably the most famous film clip in American history. And in those scant few seconds of footage virtually every element, every body, every landmark that can be seen has been scrutinized beyond all human reason. Here's the Reader's Digest timeline: forty minutes after the shots were fired Lee Harvey Oswald was arrested in a movie theater on suspicion of killing a police officer a few blocks away. He was soon after deemed the primary suspect in the killing of the president and two days later he was gunned down on national television by Dallas nightclub owner, Jack Ruby. One week after the assassination President Johnson created a President's Commission led by Supreme Court Chief Justice Earl Warren. This commission, later to be known as the Warren Commission, was charged with determining whether Lee Harvey Oswald indeed acted alone. The Commission relied on the State Department, FBI, Secret Service, CIA and the Zapruder film. The Commission's findings were that Oswald killed Kennedy all by his lonesome."

Web nods impatiently. "Yes, that's the company line. But what do you think really happened?"

Professor Aronson arches one of his boxcar brows in exaggerated curiosity. "You don't go along with the company line?"

"Well, until a few months ago, maybe, but now I'm not so sure."

"Really? And why is that?"

Web measures his words carefully. "Based on the research I've done."

The professor rocks from his chair and steps to the window, looking out over the campus. "So you don't believe Oswald, a man who was considered a lousy shot by Marine Corp standards could have gotten off the three shots in approximately eight seconds, two of them accurately in under six, using a bolt action rifle?"

"Three shots in eight seconds are doable."

"Speaking from experience?"

Web, again, measures his response. "Again, based on my research, the numerous tests that were done."

"Fair enough." The professor walks from the window, slowly pacing the floor of the office. Web imagines this is how the professor looks when he's in front of a room full of underclassmen, poking and prodding, playing devil's advocate, coaxing the students to question the facts and their preconceived notions. The professor raises a hand, index finger pointing at the ceiling like he's had an *a-ha* moment. "Do you believe over the next 90 seconds Oswald could then hide the rifle on the other end of the 6th floor of the Texas School Book Depository from which he allegedly fired, travel from his 6th floor "Sniper's Nest" down four flights of stairs, to be confronted by the building's superintendent and a police officer in the second floor lunch room sipping a Coke, appearing, according to them, "calm, cool normal, and not out of breath in any way"?

"A minute and a half is a long time."

"Perhaps. Let us move along to the infamous Magic Bullet theory. You are familiar with this?

Web takes his notes out, leafs through them and reads the information in a flat, neutral tone. "The first bullet that hit the president entered JFK's upper back, exited his throat, entered governor Connally's back, exited his chest, shattered the radius bone in his right wrist, entered his left leg, embedding itself in the thigh bone."

"Very good. What makes the bullet so magical is that if fired from the higher elevation of the School Book Depository it would have been travelling at a downward angle when it hit the president in the upper back, yet then managed to angle upward before exiting his throat, then angle back down to hit the governor in the back and wrist, then take a left hand turn before embedding in his left thigh. And of course then there's the little fact of how the bullet then was found in virtually perfect condition on governor Connally's stretcher."

"You don't sound convinced."

"I am merely stating the facts based on the Warren Commission's findings."

"Professor, so far everything you've said has been done so with, I dunno, a fair amount of sarcasm. It sounds like you're pretty convinced Oswald couldn't have fired the shots."

The professor smiles at this observation. "Really? I simply feel that all sides of an argument should be presented fairly. Conspiracy theorists should get their day in court as well. So then, let us play the other side of the argument. The evidence supporting the supposition that Oswald fired on the president is substantial." The professor sits on the corner of his desk and points a wiry finger at Web. His words burst out; projected with the air of a trial lawyer who's absolutely convinced the defendant is as guilty as Judas in the garden. "The following are assertions made in the case against Mr. Oswald." As the professor speaks he ticks each list item off on his fingers. "Number one, multiple witnesses saw Mr. Oswald, or someone who looked much like Mr. Oswald at the window of the sixth floor of the Texas School Book Depository. Two, Mr. Oswald's palm print was on the rifle. Three, Mr. Oswald's palm print was found on the cardboard box found at the window. Four, the rifle had been purchased by Mr. Oswald through the mail. Five, the bullet fragments recovered from the president's limousine were perfectly matched to Mr. Oswald's rifle using neutron activation analysis. Six, Mr. Oswald was seen in the building right after the shooting. Seven, Mr. Oswald immediately left the building, went home and changed clothes. Eight, the pistol that fired the bullets that killed the police officer near where Mr. Oswald was arrested belonged to, yes, Mr. Oswald." The professor stops and looks at his eight raised fingers. "There's plenty more but you get the idea, and besides, I'm running out of fingers." The professor climbs off the edge of the desk and settles back into his chair, tucks his elbows into his ribs and holds his hands out before him like a magician indicating nothing up his sleeve.

Web considers the professor's comments before turning his eyes back to the little man on the other side of the desk. "So, again, based on your years of research and the information you have just presented to me, do you feel Oswald killed President Kennedy?"

The professor smiles almost sadly, drawing back his hands to clasp and settle upon his belt buckle. "Mr. Weller, if I had a dollar for every time a student asked me that I could have long retired."

"And your official answer is?"

"Much to the disappointment of my students and colleagues, my official answer is that, from a purely legal perspective, I have not been presented with enough compelling evidence to convince me that someone other than Lee Harvey Oswald killed the president."

Silence. Web nods, clicks off his tape recorder, fails to get it to stop rolling, and punches it again with a little more authority than is really necessary. He closes his notebook and stands, hand outstretched. "Thank you for your time, professor."

Professor Aronson stands, shakes Web's hand and shows him to the door. As he holds the door open he reaches a thin arm across, blocking Web's escape. "Mr. Weller, you asked me what my official answer is, but you neglected to ask me what my unofficial answer is."

Web raises his comparatively feeble eyebrows in response, letting that suffice. The professor removes his glasses and polishes the lens with the loose portion of his shirt blousing up from where it is tucked into his pants. "Evidence is evidence, but there is something to be said for gut feeling. The Warren Report says Oswald acted alone in shooting Kennedy, but as they used to say in old movies, that's three day old fish and I'm not buying."

Web's eyes flick back and forth trying to decipher the professor's analogy so the little man sighs and clarifies, disappointed that his cleverness has fallen on deaf ears.

"Something about it stinks, Mr. Weller. Is there one particular fact that makes me think there were other gunmen? No. Not even the ridiculous Magic Bullet Theory.

But everything, taken as a whole..." The professor shakes his head. "I can't get past the fact that it just doesn't add up. The fish stinks, Mr. Weller, and I'm not buying."

33

Days pass. Web's attention to his Town of Heroes book dims, slowly shifting away to his Kennedy assassination research. His notebook is filling up, but he's careful to keep his papers hidden. When he first came up with the war stories book idea he was flush with excitement and pride. But this Kennedy thing has brought about a whole new sensation. One he hasn't felt since his early days in the field. It's the finger-on-the-electric-fence rush of adrenaline that only surfaces when you're balanced on the razor's edge between right and wrong. Where a butterfly's kiss can topple you in one direction or the other. He used to feel that way a lot on his early missions, staring down the barrel of his rifle, finger on the trigger, knowing with the slightest pull he would end a life, perhaps creating a widow or orphan, but telling himself that by doing so he was saving many more lives. Over time that rush tapered away due to the simple fact that the more you did it, the more missions you accomplished, the more you were absolutely convinced you were doing the right thing. It's the only way you can survive in that role. You have to know that your firing that bullet is the greatest thing that ever happened to a whole shit-load of people. You are surgically removing a cancerous tumor so that the patient may live. You are a professional doing a job to the best of your abilities and if you get an atta boy from a colleague that is the highest praise you can hope for. Web never felt he was a hero worthy of ticker-tape parades and supermodels and that countless people should be falling to their goddamn knees and thanking their lucky stars that he and his trusty rifle were yet again Johnny-on-the-fuckin-spot. But hey, if that ever happened, he'd be okay with it.

Knowing that took away some of the rush, but not all of it. Being on a mission, the feeling of accomplishment was still better than 40 year-old scotch. And that's what Web was beginning to feel with this Kennedy thing. That's what he'd taken to calling it, almost like the word "assassination" would bite him if he spoke it. He knew that was guilt speaking. The most pathetic and weak-assed emotion in the book. And, ironically, one of the most powerful. Hell, look at it what it's done to Catholics. One could argue that this one crappy little sentiment has effectively held millions of their dearly devoted hostage for over two thousand years. Most soldiers will tell you guilt is for pussies. If you fuck up, deal with it. Of course, most soldiers will also tell you it's easier said than done. Whatever you want to say about guilt, it's human nature, a natural instinct. Those who don't feel it fall into a completely different category: sociopath—someone who doesn't feel bad about screwing people over. Those folks usually ended up with their face on a poster in police stations and federal agencies. A sniper instructor that, like Web, also had a thing for science fiction writers, passed along a quote from Aldous Huxley, author of *Brave New World*, in which Web frequently found solace. To paraphrase—"Chronic remorse is a most undesirable sentiment. If you behave badly, repent and make amends. Rolling in the muck is not the best way of getting clean." In other words, when you fuck up, suck it up, try to make good and move on. Again, easier said than done, but nonetheless, good words to live by in a gunman's world. And nice to know someone as kick-ass as Aldous Huxley felt the same way.

So why was Web feeling so anxious about this Kennedy thing? As he keeps reminding himself he hasn't done anything with it. Yet. There's the operative word. Yet. That's the word Web feels is the fulcrum to his emotional seesaw. Another word that keeps trying to throw sand bags onto one side of the teeter-totter: betrayal.

The Marine's motto is Semper Fidelis, Latin for Always Faithful. It's all about honor. But Web wonders how many Marines have been faced with having to choose between honor and perhaps the most incredible story since Moses stepped off the mountain. Not to mention the instant fame and riches that will go with it. But the question may be completely moot. Did he even have a story or was he trying way too hard to find cold, hard facts where only rumor, coincidence and circumstantial evidence share a flat?

Web wonders if this is how Woodward and Bernstein felt, the reporters who uncovered the Watergate scandal. The big difference is that Woodward and Bernstein didn't give a rat's ass about Nixon and company. It was the story that mattered. And Web is hip-deep in that feeling.

And then a letter shows up.

It is from the last publisher Web had queried about his Heroes book. They feel it shows promise and piques their curiosity. They want a proposal.

The earth tilts on its axis, hell freezes over, pigs fly and rainbows and unicorns pour forth from the envelope. A publisher wants a proposal. God is good. Amen.

34

Word has spread. A publisher wants a proposal! Most residents of Little Norway aren't really sure what that means but they know it's something good. Grace has become a one woman publicist for Web, making sure everyone in town, and even a few out-of-towners who happened by the market, know that Little Norway's newly adopted son is on the verge of greatness. In Grace's version of the foreseeable future Web will soon be the darling of the literary world, he'll rub elbows with the likes of Stephen King and Lee Child (that handsome fella who writes those awesome Jack Reacher thrillers), he'll be on NBC's Today Show, Letterman will create a Top 10 list of why Web Weller is such a writing stud (#6—He's a man of letters all right, he told all publishers who snubbed him FU), he'll meet the president, tabloids will connect him with all number of Hollywood starlets and he'll snag People magazine's title of Sexiest Man Alive.

Web's back is sore from the congratulatory slaps, he's packed on another five pounds from the flood of brownies and lemon bars and his smile is back. His smile is most definitely back. Web thinks being on a Letterman Top 10 list would be cool as hell.

35

Merry-go-rounds, or carousels, were at their
heyday in the U.S. in the late 1800's through the first couple
of decades of the 1900's. Riders put on their Sunday best
to hit the carnival midways and ride the ornately carved
menagerie of beasts. Carousel operators, no chumps at
marketing, came up with a way to give their riders a little
bonus to the ride. It was the brass ring. Hung just within
reach, if your horse rose up at precisely the right moment,
you could attempt to grab the brass ring, which, if your
attempt was successful, would result in a prize, usually
another free ride. The term *Grab the Brass Ring* soon
became part of the American lexicon, a phrase to describe
going for it. And everyone cheers for the one who goes for
it and is rewarded for his perseverance. That's the hero in
the movie, the guy who pulls himself up by his bootstraps,
shows some pluck and keeps going when the going gets
tough. It's David kicking Goliath's ass and everyone loves
David.

But there's a downside to going for it. The side that
usually doesn't make the evening papers or get made
into movies. It's the decidedly more common outcome:
the swing and a miss. But the brave or hardheaded swing
anyway because they feel the reward is worth the risk.

Winners see success, losers see failure and when you're within reach of a dream, when it's so close you can see its pores and smell its delicious aroma it's so easy to envision the spoils of success. You see victory! You see success! That's why when you're on the merry-go-round and the brass ring is right there—it's right there!—if you reach and miss and your momentum carries you off the horse's back, the fall can be infinitely more painful. But, of course, the solution is simple—just don't miss.

36

Web is comfortably flopped on Pa's couch with a bowl of cereal. He's said to hell with the bran and has crossed back over to the dark side: Cocoa Puffs. He flips on the TV and munches away. *Entertainment Tonight* is on, which means Web's brain is off. It is a day off of sorts. No interviews, no research, just a day to relax.

On the television the bubbly host talks about their exclusive coverage of some big media event. They cut to their equally bubbly reporter in the field. It's some sort of red carpet affair in a swank Los Angeles hotel. The reporter goes on about what a star-studded event it is and nabs a celebrity walking by. Web nearly drops his spoon when he sees it's Sal Shelby. He's in a tux, drinking Champagne. The overly pert reporter stands tall. "Ladies and gentlemen, I just caught world-renowned author, Sal Shelby. Having a good time, Sal?"

Sal flashes his 100-watt smile and gives a practiced wink to the camera. "Terrific! Having a ball!"

Web looks at Sal in his tux and cocktail, and then looks down at his ratty self, eating cereal on a threadbare couch.

The reporter shifts gears, dropping perky in favor of a more dignified vibe. "I understand you have a new book coming out on your experience in Afghanistan while you were with the Marine Corp."

Sal mirrors the reporter's more serious demeanor. "Yes, should hit bookstores next month."

"And I understand there's already talk of turning it into a movie."

"That's correct. They're actually in talks with Ryan Gosling about playing, well, me."

Web smiles at the scene. *That can be me. Web Weller on ET talking about which A-List actor will play me when my latest, greatest book is optioned.* Grace's optimism has rubbed off on him but good. He has just glimpsed a scene of what his life can soon be and it looks pretty damn fine.

At this moment the front door flies open and Holly darts in. She's very excited, out of breath, like she ran a considerable distance. "There you are! Grace wanted me to deliver this letter to you! It's from the publisher."

Web takes the letter from her. He's trying to look outwardly cool, but his excitement is one degree short of boiling over. The envelope is rectangular and bone white but to Web it is round and brass. And right there.

He fumbles with the envelope, tearing at the flap. The envelope finally springs open. Web steps away to read the letter within.

The usually cool Holly can barely keep from bouncing on her toes with anticipation. "Well? What did they say?"

The merry-go-round slowly turns and the brass ring appears from around the bend, shining brightly, full of promise. And the ring is right there. Web sees his failures, his doubts, his frustrations all poised to vaporize like a target city under a nuke. Poof. Now you see it, now you don't. He reaches out, almost casually (because it's right there!) and closes his hand around the cold, shiny metal. He couldn't miss it if he tried. Winners see success!

Web reads the letter.

Mr. Weller, upon further consideration, we are sorry to inform you that...

The ring is gone. Web's hand clutches at dead air. His mind reels, trying to make sense of the sudden reality shift. Mighty Casey has struck out. There is no joy in Mudville today. The brass ring that was there now flat out isn't. It's like climbing stairs and misjudging a step. Your body is prepared for your foot to land and when you miss you tumble forward, your balance sent packing, your hands spontaneously reaching out for the railing, looking for something to keep you from doing a face plant in the upper steps. But there are no railings, nothing to grasp onto. There is only negative space and you fall.

Web turns to face Holly, a subtle shake of his head tells the story. The news physically deflates Holly. "I'm sorry. Maybe next time."

From his mother's side Web is infused with a thoughtful nature, from his father, stoicism, or, as some would say, a lack of emotion of Scandinavian proportions. As a result Web Weller has never been a man prone to outburst. On one occasion, while Web was working out in a public gym, quietly going about his business, halfway through a set of curls, a man began to badger him for no apparent reason. In hindsight the man had to be a whack-job or off his meds, but at that moment he was just an asshole who wouldn't shut up. When Web asked the man what his problem was the man insisted Web was his problem and continued to heckle Web mercilessly. The verbal assault was so random, so completely unprovoked that it short circuited Web's rational brain. The human mind is trained through experience and repetition to respond to circumstances consistent with societal norms and natural expectations. If A then B. If a friend gives you a gift you say thank you. If you bump into someone you say excuse me. If you drop something you try to grab it. So when you don't get the prescribed response it throws you. Being read the riot act by a stranger in a public place for no apparent reason pretty much threw a wrench in Web's cognitive machinery.

Web could have walked away, that would have been the smart move, the rational move, the move you would encourage your children to make, but the man's verbal attack was so nutso, so completely out of nowhere and so relentless that normal reaction didn't figure into the equation. Web snapped. He saw red, and soon after saw blue, as in the cops. The moral of the story is every person has a line and you never know where that line is until it gets crossed. Then all bets are off. You do things you normally wouldn't do—normally would be ashamed of—and you really don't give a shit until much later. It's a lesson you would think we'd learn once we got bit with consequences, but as Spock from *Star Trek* always liked to accurately point out humans are messy, illogical emotional things. When we're pissed we have a tendency to forget about consequences and jump in with both feet without bothering to ask about how deep the water is.

This is the mother of one of those moments. The invisible line got crossed. Web has reached for his dream, he has missed, he has failed and he has fallen. And it hurts. Bad. And what do we do when we are hurt? We lash out; we strike back, regardless of what we are taught at our mother's knee. And the more you hurt the harder you want to hit the bastard who hurt you. Metaphor-wise, Web is ready to counterpunch with one sumbitch of a haymaker.

U.S. Marine Corp Snipers aren't supposed to be like that, they are trained to be cool and calm under any circumstance but at this moment Web Weller doesn't give a shit.

Web turns on Holly, his voice a shout. "Next time? What next time?"

Holly is taken aback by his sudden anger and tries to mollify him. "I'm just saying that maybe another publisher will..."

"Will what? Kick me in the teeth again?" Web's anger only intensifies. "Just do me a favor and shut the hell up. This is what I get for hanging my hopes on a bunch of small town losers."

Now it's Holly's turn to get pissed off. "Losers? Who's the loser? How dare you talk about these people like that? They took you in when you didn't have a pot to piss in or a window to throw it out of. These are proud, honorable people who've at least accomplished something in their lives. What the hell have you done?"

"Me? What about you? The small town girl who

wants to travel to the big city but doesn't have the guts. What have you accomplished, other than being the town tramp?"

"What?!!"

"You've been practically throwing yourself at me because I'm the closest thing to the big time that you've ever seen."

"You're dreaming if you think you got a chance with me!" She storms into her bedroom and comes out with her rifle, then takes off the shorts she was wearing right in front of him and proceeds to pull on a pair of jeans. She makes sure he gets a good look at her long legs before she stomps out the door. At the landing she stops and turns on him one last time with a look of utter contempt. "God, you are such a dick," and slams the door.

Web silently bristles. Soon he's pacing and eventually his anger boils over and he storms into his bedroom and flops down onto the bed. He curses the publisher, curses the town, curses Sal-fucking-Shelby. He stops and rereads the letter aloud. "We are sorry to inform you that we feel the subject matter you propose is not something we are interested in pursuing at this time." He balls up the letter and throws it across the tiny room. "What the hell do you need to get someone's attention?" he fairly shouts to the ceiling. At that moment he stops, trying to get a grip on his emotions. He rises from the bed and steps out into the main room. He looks at the door to the storage room. The room where he found the box of mysterious stuff weeks earlier. He goes to the door, creeps inside and heads straight for the box where he found the photo of Helen, the train ticket and the film reels. He takes out a reel and fits it onto the old projector that's still sitting on the card table in the middle of the room. His anger still running the Daytona 500 through his body, it takes him a minute to figure out how to thread the ancient projector and once the film rolls another few minutes to realize what he's seeing.

In sniper school, hell, in just about any branch of the military you become overly familiar with what reconnaissance video looks like. It's not sexy, it's not artistic, there are no clever camera moves. The purpose of the video is to give the viewer a clear understanding of the objective. Sight lines, obstructions, traffic, crowd congestion, anything that can offer intelligence. To anyone else the film flickering on the screen might look like home movies shot by a tourist on vacation, but Web sees more than that. There are no smiling family members waving in the foreground, no shots of anything that might be generally deemed memorable. The clips are systematic in their framing and order: wide static shot of the entire grounds, followed by a slow pan from left to right, then back from right to left. Then medium close ups of all noticeable objects: park benches, freeway signs, a pool, a pergola perched atop a low grassy hill. Lastly close ups of everything already shot. Then the film jumps to the same series of shots but from a different location, the opposite point of view. Lastly, from another location, 45 degrees from the two previous spots. Triangulation.

Web has never been there but he's seen enough archival footage on newscasts over the years to recognize where this film was shot: Dealey Plaza in Dallas: the grounds where Kennedy was shot.

Web picks up the film canister and looks at the initials printed on it. DP. Web quietly reads it to himself. "DP. Dealey Plaza." The faded image on the old screen shows the infamous grassy knoll. The train trestle in the distance. The Texas School Book Depository where Lee Harvey Oswald allegedly took the fatal shots. Web shuts down the projector and quickly removes the reel, stuffing it back into the box from whence it came. Web stares and quietly growls at the box, "The Warren Commission was full of shit."

Web storms back into his small bedroom. His anger has dialed back a smidge but is still hovering on the fringes of Critical Mass. His eyes are red, he's unshaven; frankly he looks like hell and feels about the same. He picks up the balled up rejection letter and flattens it out on the bedspread. While staring at the wrinkled, traitorous letter he picks up his tape recorder and peers in at the tiny reel. Almost out of tape. He takes a moment to collect his thoughts and dictates harshly into the built in microphone. "Final publisher's response concerning A Town of Heroes. *The subject matter you propose is not something we are interested in pursuing at this time.*" Web throws himself backward onto the bed again and stares blankly at the ceiling. After a moment he sits back up and rises from the bed. He goes for his duffle bag, which in all the time he's been living there he's still not completely unpacked. He takes out the small wooden box that holds his family photos and carefully removes the one of him and his dad with the buck. He draws a finger across the photo before coming to rest on the image of his father.

In Web's eyes Nicholas Turk Weller was the most patriotic man in America. He drives a Ford, always buys American, votes Republican, thinks The Mick was the greatest ballplayer of all time, believes John Wayne was the second coming, smoked Luckys (until he kicked the habit after his heart gave a flutter, scaring the bejeezus out of him), drinks Miller Hi-Life or Wild Turkey, married his high-school sweetheart—it didn't take, but he got a son to show for it—married a second time, better results, had Web! He is a devout Presbyterian unless the church service conflicts with a ballgame, and walked himself straight down to the Marine recruiter's office on his eighteenth birthday so he could go to strange new lands, meet exotic people...and shoot them. He was commissioned a lieutenant in the Corp and given an honorable medical discharge eighteen months later after taking three bullets in the ass, one of which severed his sciatic nerve. The identical wound, he likes to point out, that took Hollywood tough guy Lee Marvin off the battlefield in World War II. He hunted elk with a Browning A-Bolt 338 Win Mag until it got too easy and he switched to a bow. He reads the newspaper every morning and watches the 11 o'clock news every night. If he has any skeletons in his closet that closet is locked tight and the key tossed in a river. To the best of Web's knowledge his father could run for any office in politics and his opponent wouldn't be able to scrape up a single handful of mud. And Nick Weller can talk politics with the best of them. The man is never short of an opinion and will stand by his principles come hell or high water. He believes Capitol Hill is littered with cheats and swindlers but believes too that, despite those bad apples, our government is still the best government in the world. He is generous with his time, not so much with his money. He recycles religiously, not because it's politically correct but because it seems like a good idea. He owns one suit and three ties: one red, one blue, one striped. If it were up to him he'd wear jeans or sweats seven days a week. He likes his steaks medium rare and his baked potatoes with just butter, no sour cream, bacon or any of that chives shit. He loves to work with his hands. Loves to lift, pound, sand, or simply tinker. He can swear a blue streak when around the guys but never in front of women. The greatest insult he can lay upon another is to say they're lazy. He played catcher in baseball and middle linebacker in football through high school. He can describe with microscopic detail everything about his most heroic moments behind the plate (Overcast, home game, 4 for 5 with a double and a 392-foot home run to left center—he stepped it off after the game—against arch-rival Parrish High) or on the grid-iron (34 degrees, sleet, away game, twelve tackles, two sacks, one a blindside hit that put Winston High's pretty boy AllState quarterback out for the rest of the season). Nick Weller never could play basketball to save his life. He is loyal until you wrong him and he will not abide a hand being laid upon him. He expects sales people, strangers and anyone substantially younger than him to refer to him as Mr. or sir. He is loving, proud and he is unforgiving.

Web stares at the image of his father. "Talk to me, you son of a bitch."

Web places the photo back inside the wood box, punches the off button on the recorder and carries it into the main room. He absentmindedly sets the recorder down on the table and does a quick check around the house to make sure both Pa and Holly are gone before slipping back inside his own room. He places his Town of Heroes notebook on the bed and then takes out the manila folder that he's had hidden under his mattress. He begins sifting through the pages of notes. Kennedy, Dealey Plaza, Pa's secret film, the train ticket, Pa's sniper background. He places the manila envelope on the bed next to the notebook and stares them down. After a moment Web stands and paces as much as his tiny room allows, which is about three steps in any one direction. He walks back out into the main room and grabs the phone. He quickly punches in a number.

37

Sal Shelby is cuffing an expensive ivory colored dress shirt while he cradles the phone under his chin. He's obviously getting ready to go somewhere high-rent, even though it's morning. "Yello."

Back in Pa's house Web stands before the fireplace, perfectly serious and composed, the exact opposite of Sal's upbeat tone. Web has rerouted his anger. He's on a mission. He thinks of Clint Eastwood in the movie *Heartbreak Ridge*, where Clint the Squint plays a Master Gunnery Sergeant constantly driving his sad sack group of recruits to A*dapt, Improvise, Overcome!* In other words, have a Plan-B.

Web is cashing in his Plan-B. "Sal, it's Web."

"Web? What's up, my brutha? Long time!"

"Sal, I've got something for your publisher. Something very big. Very special. I'd like you to pass it along to him."

"For you? The world. But it better be good."

"I'd bet my life on it."

"How melodramatic. I like it already! So, you gonna tell me or do I gotta guess? You know I don't have any patience."

"All I'm going to tell you is that it's earth shattering stuff."

"Okay, fine, play coy. So where are you anyway?"

"I'm in a town called Little Norway. It's in Minnesota. Somewhere just outside of Bum Fuck, Egypt."

"How the hell did you find something 'earth shattering' out there?"

"You wouldn't believe me if I told you. I'll keep you posted. See ya."

Sal stares at the dead phone in his hand looking utterly perplexed. After a moment's consideration he dials 411. "Yeah, I need the phone number for Midwest Airlines."

38

Web steps back into his room. He never notices that the tape recorder that he'd set on the table in the main room never shut off. The Duracell double A's stream enough juice for the reels to continue silently rolling. Web puts the notes back in the large manila envelope and slips it back under the bed. He sits on the edge of the bed, still cool and composed, but finally his head lowers into his hands. After a moment he sits back up and looks around, seemingly at a loss as to what to do. He spots his rifle, grabs it and his coat and heads out. As Web walks out the front door the tape recorder continues to roll. After a second the tape runs out and the recorder clicks itself off.

39

Holly is sitting on a log by the drifter's tent, drawing in the dirt with a stick. She's agitated. No, she's seriously pissed. That whole blow up with Web has left her with a severe case of the Fuck Yous. She's not completely sure why she came here. Normally when she is fired up about something she goes to Grace. Grace has a way of settling her down without being patronizing. But this time Holly's feet took her into the woods, to the campsite of a stranger. Perhaps that's why she came there, because this man has no connection to Little Norway and its peculiarities. He is indifferent to its ways and means. Well, other than perhaps holding a bit of a grudge for having a gun leveled at him by a senior citizen. The point being he has no stake in Web Weller's success or failure. He has no dog in this fight.

The drifter sips coffee and watches her. "You look... upset."

Holly responds with a stare that could cut glass, catches herself and softens. "I'm just pissed."

"About what?"

"Nothing. Little Norway stuff."

The drifter smiles. "Now what could possibly happen in this beautiful oasis of rural charm and good-will-toward-men that could make you mad?"

Holly's eyes turn icy again at his sarcasm but she soon grins in spite of herself. "It's nothing. I'll get over it."

The drifter sees he's not going to get more from her on the subject and shrugs it off. After a sip of coffee he does a little conversational end-around. "So, you happy here in your little paradise?"

Holly responds a little too quickly, too snappish to sound convincing. "It's great. I can hunt, fish, hike."

"What about the outside world?

"It's not like I'm in a bubble. I'm home-schooled by Gracie and get to use her computer whenever I want. We've got satellite TV. I got a cellphone." She glances up to see his slightly incredulous expression. "Believe it or not I actually have heard of Kim Kardashian and Justin Timberlake."

The drifter holds his hands up in acquiescence. He's quiet for a moment, takes another sip of coffee and finally turns to her with a thoughtful gaze. "Would you like to get away?"

"Get away?"

"Yeah. Travel. See some of those things you've only seen on TV and the Internet."

"I will. Someday."

"How about now?" He toes the dirt with his boot. "With me."

"What do you mean?"

"I've been traveling by myself a long time now. I don't really have any family and I could use the company. Especially company as pretty as yourself." At this Holly actually blushes. She's excited by the prospect, excited but hesitant. He can see the hesitancy. "Imagine. New York, Boston, Los Angeles."

"Paris?"

"I love Paris."

"You've been there?"

"Couple of times. Beautiful. Romantic. And the museums, the architecture, the parties, the fashion!"

By this point Holly's eyes are as big as saucers, but she physically rechecks herself.

"My family's here."

He shrugs and decides not to push it. Just smiles. "Oh well, just a thought."

40

Web is hiking along a rocky ridge, overlooking the forest. He still looks all business, but there's something more, a look of consternation. He's carrying on a conversation with himself. "It's the right thing. This is finally my chance. It's what I've always wanted." Web peers through his rifle sight, spots something and fires. The mere act of firing the gun soothes him.

41

The Drifter looks from Holly off into the trees.
"So you're telling me your family just lets you wander around the wilderness by yourself?"

Holly just looks at him like he's nuts. City boy. "Duh. I'd sure as hell trust myself out in these woods more than you."

"Yet I've managed to live out here for weeks without any problem. Looks like the city boy's done all right for himself."

"If you ask me you've just been lucky. Lucky somebody else hasn't figured out it's you who's camping here."

"Whatever. So far so good."

"How do you get along? Foodwise, I mean. You're not hunting, that I'm sure of."

"I do what every good American does, I shop."

"Not in Little Norway."

"Believe it or not there are more than a few stores that will gladly take my money outside of Little Norway. There's a little convenience store a few miles outside of town that I drop by regularly. It's not too far a walk. Occasionally I hitchhike. Me and the kid working the counter, big sci-fi buff, we've become pretty good buds."

"What, you mean you don't just steal stuff when you

need it?"

The drifter gives her look like that's not such a big deal. "Only in a pinch. When you're on the road you do what you gotta do to get by."

"So you're saying you've stolen other stuff from people in Little Norway?"

The drifter turns his hands out and rolls his eyes like, again, it's no big deal. "Here and there. Little stuff. They'll probably never notice."

Holly shakes her head with a look completely barren of understanding. "You just don't get it, do you? That shit does not fly in this town. And I am not kidding even a little bit."

The drifter flutters his hand like he's waving away flies. "Yeah, whatever. No harm, no foul."

Holly continues to look at him like he's crazy. "You're lucky somebody hasn't stumbled across your campsite or recognized you while you're hitchhiking."

"I'll give you that I've been a little lucky someone hasn't found my campsite, other than you I mean. But I guess luck is part of the game."

"Part of the game? Is that what this is to you? A game?"

"Yeah, I guess, a little. Sort of like hide-and-seek. Of course, I got one thing going for me."

"And what's that?"

"Pretty much you and gun-toting Grace are the only ones in Little Norway who've seen me up close and personal. Well, the only ones who could match me up with that little incident at Grace's store."

"I'm surprised anyone picks you up when you're hitchhiking. Folks around here aren't high on drifters coming into town."

"I hitchhike heading *out* of town. People seem more than willing to give me a ride away from their little burg. I try to change up my look in case I'm spotted by the same people on more than one occasion. I hitchhike out of town but I walk back, and when I do I try to stay off the main road. Travel a lot at night. Your town's small but not so small that a stranger occasionally walking along the road is cause for alarm. Frankly, the whole cloak and dagger thing has been kind of fun."

"If you like to travel around so much why stay here? Out in the woods near a town where most residents would just as soon kick your ass for trying to rip off Grace."

The drifter thinks on that for a brief moment. "I don't like being told what to do."

"That's it?" says Holly, incredulously, "You don't like being told what to do? You kidding me?"

"When your friend Grace aimed her gun at me and told me to get lost I almost did. But then I thought *Screw you.* This is a free country. You can't make me go just because you don't like me."

"Yeah, actually they can. And they will."

"All the more reason for me to stay. And I did. Well, for a little while. After the thing at the market I kind of hunkered down for a few days. Different campsite, about a quarter mile from here. Basically I just stewed, pissed off, and licked my wounds, as it were. Finally I said the hell with this place and split. Went up north, found a couple of other towns and milled about, but I kept thinking *Screw you, Little Norway!* You can't make me leave. So I came back."

"How long have you holed up here?"

"Oh, around a month or so. And no one's been the wiser."

Holly can't argue the point. To the best of her knowledge he's right, no one seems to know he is out there. No one but her.

The drifter aims a subtle smile Holly's way. "So why haven't you told anyone about me?"

Holly doesn't answer. She goes back to drawing in the dirt with the stick.

The drifter tips his head back slightly, kind of an *A-ha* look. "Because knowing I'm out here is exciting, isn't it?"

Holly continues to scribble the dirt, purposefully avoiding his eye contact.

The drifter picks up and pitches a small rock into the middle of her artwork. Holly's eyes reflexively dart up to his.

"That's it, isn't it? Me being out here is dangerous. Coming to see me out here even more so."

Right at this moment they hear a gunshot in the distance. The shot startles the drifter. Holly hardly notices.

"What was that?"

Holly shrugs. "I dunno. Probably another hunter."

The drifter takes notice of Holly's rifle in her hands. "Can I see your gun?"

"It's not a gun, it's a rifle."

"Okay, so it's a rifle. May I see your rifle? Pretty please, with sugar?"

Holly gives him a hard stare. "You want it? Gonna have to take it."

The drifter stops, unsure how to respond to her sudden seriousness. After a beat Holly breaks into a grin. "I'm kidding. Geez, you city folk are gullible." She hands over her rifle.

He looks it over admiringly. "Nice."

"Nice? It's beautiful."

Holly watches the drifter turning the gun over in his hand. She can tell just by the way he's holding it, like it's some puzzling curiosity, that it very well could be the first time he's held one. She nods at the gun. "You don't own one?"

The drifter scrunches his face up like he'd just downed a slug of sour milk. "Me? Nah. Never saw the need."

Holly blinks at him like he is speaking in tongues. "Never saw the need? I thought you said you traveled all over?"

"I have."

"Just big cities?"

"Hardly. Backpacked through Alaska. Lived in a tent in Cordova for two months. Rained almost the whole time." The drifter can see he's scoring some points with the young woman. He piles on. "I've hitchhiked across Canada, slept in train boxcars, barns. Hell, I even slept in a doghouse."

Holly grins. "Must have been for a pretty big frickin' dog. Bull Mastiff or something."

The drifter returns the smile and nods. He looks back at the forgotten gun in his hands and gingerly hands it back. Holly accepts the rifle, props it against the log she's sitting on and turns a quizzical look his way. "So you've roamed around the world, slept in ditches, gotten rides from complete strangers, always been the outsider and you never thought you needed a gun? Just for protection?"

The drifter gives her a *who-cares* shrug. "Never been a gun guy. I mean, they're kind of cool in a TV show and movies kind of way, but I don't really get 'em."

He might as well have said the Pope had a porno collection by the look on Holly's face. She instantly understood why heretics and blasphemers were burned at the stake in olden times. "What, are you fuckin' stupid?"

The drifter isn't sure what is more startling to him, the sudden curse word uttered by the lovely young woman in front of him or the complete and utter sincerity in her expression. He feels like he just stepped on an upturned rake and took the handle right in the chops. His mind races, looking for a save. "Well, it's just that, uh..." He eyes flash to his backpack lying by the front flap of the tent. He holds up a finger in a *hold that thought* manner. He steps over to the pack and draws out a rectangular-ish black shape. He hands it to Holly. It's a military folding knife; the blade safely tucked up inside the contoured black plastic handle. Holly folds out the thick blade with a snick as the base locks in place. The business end is a good four inches of stainless steel; nearly half of it sporting brutal serrated teeth. From stem to stern, the knife's eight inches of lethal American craftsmanship.

Holly looks it over, inspecting it like a museum curator appraising a framed oil, brushed by a Dutch Master. Her appreciation is evident.

"That's a good knife." She presses the circular release button and eases the blade back into the handle before handing it back.

The drifter takes a relieved breath, glad for returning to her good graces. "Thanks. It's come in handy."

"I don't doubt. Where'd you get it?"

"I, uh..." The drifter's pause is just long enough to tell the story.

Holly shakes her head, but with a smile. "Uh, huh, what I thought. You stole it." She gives him a look of *some people never learn.*

The drifter smiles back. Busted, but not badly. In all his travels if he has learned one thing about people—young women, in particular—it's keep them in their comfort zone. Talk football with guys in hardhats, chat about children with parents, and you can't go wrong conversing about music with teenagers. But it hadn't taken him long to see Holly was not your average teenager. He didn't see her as the type endlessly texting the latest gossip with her girlfriends. This was a young woman of unique interests. One such interest propped next to her. He nods at the rifle.

"Why do you like guns so much?"

She thinks on that for a second before turning a direct gaze on him. "I think they're hot." Her directness flusters him. His flustering makes her smile. "Here." She reaches under her coat and removes a large pistol from a shoulder holster. She tosses him the pistol. He holds the pistol like it's hot. He gradually gets more comfortable with it, aims at a tree and pretends to fire. Holly enjoys watching him, like watching a kid with a new, unfamiliar toy. "Go ahead, pull the trigger." He does but nothing happens. She smiles. "It's not loaded, dummy." She reaches into her shirt pocket and pulls out a shell, tosses it to him. "You wanna shoot something?"

He looks at the gun, then at her. "Yes."

She steps over and takes the gun from him, takes aim at a tree about twenty feet away and promptly takes off a limb with a direct hit. She offers him back the gun. He draws a bead on the same tree and fires, missing completely, as if no shell had left the gun's barrel.

"Wow," says Holly, "I think that's about the most embarrassing thing I've ever seen in my life. How can you miss a tree from this distance? I could probably throw a rock and hit it."

Holly can tell her words sting the drifter more than she's anticipated. *Must be one of those sensitive guys.* She quickly tries to make amends by stepping over to him, standing close, less than arm's reach. He doesn't step back. Holly slowly reaches over, taking his hand holding the pistol. She circles around behind him drawing his other hand up to the pistol, helping him sight down the barrel while her head is right up close alongside his. She can feel the stubble from his scruff of beard draw across her cheek; hear his deepening breaths. He fires. Twenty feet away a gnarled branch explodes. The sharp, deep crack of the gunshot rolls out from the campsite, quickly escaping through a clearing and racing on into the neighboring hills.

He was right. His living here is dangerous. Her knowing he was here, even more so. And she loved it. It was like a triple shot of espresso, followed by a two-liter of Mountain Dew and a handful of No Doze. On a ridge about a half mile from her home, she could just make out the campsite through a break in the trees. She would come out with her rifle and use her scope like a pair of binoculars, peering down on his pathetic tent, occasionally spotting him struggling with his ridiculous fire or simply stretched out reading a book. She loved the fact that his presence was her personal secret. That one word from her and he'd be, at the very least, ushered off his campsite with extreme prejudice. She held his fate in her hands and it was wonderful.

On the hike out here her adrenaline raced and her heart hammered in her chest. She was beyond pissed at Web but there was something more driving her emotions. She had only visited a handful of times, always innocently. She purposefully never came more than once every week or two, which kept her hormonal stove burning merrily along. But the devil on her shoulder was growing impatient. She felt like one of those Acapulco cliff divers standing at the brink, waiting for the tide to rush in so that the water would be deep enough when she broke the surface. When she'd reached around to help him hold the pistol the tide had rushed in. When the gun fires, she leaps.

With no warning, she turns and kisses the drifter hard,

violently. She breaks away just long enough to tell him... "If you want it, you're gonna have to take it." He pauses, unsure again. But this time her face doesn't change. "I'm not kidding."

That's all it takes.

He grabs her and drags her down to the forest floor, clumsily tearing at her clothes. She's fighting him, but in that way that good girls do when they're tired of being good girls and feel they need to put up a token resistance to justify their walk of shame the following morning. Neither of them pays any attention to the gunshots in the not-too-far-distance.

42

Several spent shells lie about Web's feet. He's perched on a rock outcropping on a high ridge, sitting on a boulder that has graciously weathered over the course of millennia to a height equal to the back of Web's knee. In other words the perfect height for a chair. It's the first time he's been to this site but, judging by the thin trail leading to the outcropping, it's been visited regularly before. Initials scratched into the stone's surface verify this: HC. Holly Concannon, Web presumes. Must be one of her hide-a-ways.

Web is taking target practice. He's never been one to fire from a sitting position but the damn rock is such a perfect height he goes with it. His scope scans the trees, looking for a new target. The scope is his sanctuary: life compartmentalized in the most literal sense. When staring through this tube the only thing that matters is what you can see through the other end. He draws a bead on a broken tree trunk a few hundred yards down slope. The scorched gray skin and skeletal branches suggests the tree was at the business end of a lightning strike at some point in its past. Web squares up the center of the trunk and fires. A puff of exploding wood and dust indicates a direct hit. Web's mind and body are slipping into mission mode.

He pans right, acquiring a second target, a thick, moss-covered stump. His eye refocuses to make up the added distance and triggers off a second round. Web 2, stumps 0. He begins to quicken the pace, falling into a training method he used to refer to as acquire and fire—speedily moving his sights from one target to the next. Fire, move, fire, move, fire move. Web felt it helped him *keep in the moment* and allowed his body to move on instinct instead of being bogged down in thought—imperative in a hot combat zone. Literally fire first, ask questions later.

After three quick shots his scope passes over something that freezes his trigger finger, something not of the forest, something decidedly manmade—a tent. In that instant he pulls the rifle from his shoulder and curses himself for his recklessness. These are public grounds. It's the backwoods to be sure but the stray hiker still creeps through on occasion. He realizes his anger, frustration, and hell, he has to admit it, his guilt has affected his judgment. A cold rush of shame and embarrassment charges through his body, more from stupidly firing into open country than anything else at the moment. He draws the scope back to his eye to re-find the tent he'd just spotted. The tent is a dark green so it takes him a moment to spot it.

Human eyesight, though not in the same ballpark as that of many other creatures, is still pretty remarkable. What we lose in distance and sensitivity we make up in clarity and color. The human eye captures about 24 images a second, just like a motion picture film camera, and we perceive the whole spectrum of light—we see all the colors (except, of course, folks like Paul Newman). While dogs and cats can see much better in the dark, and at a greater distance, they see less definition and limited color. Reds appear black; greens and yellows look gray or white. However, one thing all sighted beings have in common is the visual attraction to motion. Our eyes are attracted to movement. And at that instant, Web Weller sees movement. The movement is two people struggling, a man on top, a woman on the bottom. The struggle is heated, frantic, the bodies rolling about on the dirt in front of the tent. The figures come to rest for a split second, the man back on top pinning the woman's arms down beside her head. Her shirt is halfway torn open, her back arching, her chest visibly heaving in panic. In that moment Web sees that the woman is Holly. Something else also catches Web's attention, something besides the movement: a color: a yellow patch on her attacker's shoulder. The drifter. With no hesitation Web racks a new bullet into the chamber, sights and fires.

43

Holly rolls onto her back, her wrists pinned by the drifter's weight, both their faces flushed with the sudden released sexual tension. As she arches her back, forcing her hips against his, thrilling at the sheer rush of the moment, Holly closes her eyes. When she reopens them nothing makes sense. The drifter's weight has lifted, his grip nonexistent, his face no longer staring down at hers, replaced instead by a clear view of the sky and a fine, pink mist. It takes her all of a second to register the tail end of the booming sound that until now she had always found so familiar, so reassuring—the sound of a gunshot. She senses warmth on her face, a coppery taste on her lips and reaches up with her now free hand for inspection. She wipes at her face and draws her hand away only to see it streaked a grisly red. The body of the drifter topples backwards and to the side, the smiling green peas staring blindly up from the faded yellow patch on his shoulder into Holly's unbelieving face. She kicks the still straddling lifeless body off of her and then the screaming begins.

44

Web sprints through the woods, calculating the location of the campsite on the fly, all the while turning over the events from moments ago in his head. As he draws near he can hear Holly's high-pitched screams. He pinpoints the location and rushes through the trees, yelling out her name. Seconds later he bursts into the campsite clearing. Holly is huddled by the tent, hysterical. The body of the drifter lies twisted in the dirt a few feet away. Holly's hands are caged in front of her face, her fingertips trembling against her forehead and cheeks. When she sees Web with his rifle in hand her eyes go wide and her face twists into a horror movie scream. "Murderer! You killed him!"

Web's feet turn to cement. He stops in his tracks, completely taken aback. "He...he was attacking you! I saw it!" He breaks free of his paralysis and rushes to the drifter's body, doing a quick check for a pulse and pat down. Force of habit. He finds the drifter's knife, looks it over and tosses it on the crumpled corpse.

Holly staggers forward, stripes of dust and grit clinging to her cheeks from the tears. "He wasn't attacking me!" She snatches up her guns from the ground. "I was attacking him!" She glares murderously at Web for a beat, then snaps up her rifle and aims it purposely at the center of his chest and then just as suddenly she sprints off into the woods.

45

Fifteen minutes later Web bursts through the front door of Pa's house. Pa is standing at the sink in the kitchen, drying a bowl with a hand towel. It only takes a second for Pa to see by Web's stricken face that all is not well in Little Norway.

"Web, what's wrong?"

Web stumbles forward, pitching and weaving as though he'd just finished a fifth of his dad's Wild Turkey. He drops his gun to the floor as if it were the least important object on earth. That in and of itself tells Pa some serious shit has gone down.

Web drops himself into one of the dinette chairs like a puppet who's just had his strings cut. The face he raises to Pa is not that of a former Marine sniper but of a terrified child. "I just killed a man."

Pa sets the bowl aside and quickly moves to take the chair opposite Web. "What are you talking about?"

Web is shaking his head; his words come out in a staccato. "He was attacking Holly. He was. At least I thought..."

"Who? Who was attacking Holly?"

Web relates the whole ugly mess. Pa listens with a quiet, almost clinical reserve, interrupting occasionally to get clarity on a fact here and there. By the end Web is slumped, nearly comatose in the chair. Pa slowly rises and walks to the front door, retrieving his own rifle that's propped against the jam. He bolts open the chamber, seems satisfied with the fact that it's loaded and opens the door. He turns back to Web. "You stay put until I get back."

Web rouses from his stupor and leaps to his feet. "Where are you going?"

"Don't you never mind, just stay here until I get back."

"But let me come with you! I'll need to explain to the police what happened."

Pa raises a hand and gently rests it against Web's chest. "Listen to me, Web. I need you to stay here until I get back, do you hear me? There's nothing you can do right now that can help the situation. Just stay put."

A defiant response rises and just as quickly dies in Web's throat when he sees the look in Pa's eyes. It's a look he's seen before. A look he's had before. It's the look of a man on a mission. Focused, assured, determined.

46

Web's lying on the couch in the living room, staring at the ceiling when Pa quietly walks in the front door. Web springs to his feet. "Well? Did you find Holly?"

"No, just the body of that fella you shot. It's taken care of."

"What do you mean, *taken care of?*"

"Nothing you need concern yourself with. I gotta see to a few more things. Stay put." Pa leaves.

Web frets and paces, feeling utterly helpless. He stomps into his room and flops onto the bed. He's struggling with his emotions, doing his best to keep them in check. His mind races back to the shot he took in the Middle East, the shot that cost him his career. He flashes to the image of the drifter pinning Holly to the forest floor and his instinctual reaction. He flashes to Pa. His kindness and consideration, taking Web in, treating him like a son, tying his tie for him fergawdsake! Web's mind rushes to his notes on the Kennedy assassination and Professor Aronson's unofficial thoughts on the lone gunman theory. Web thinks of the film of Dealey Plaza, the train ticket, Pa's mysterious military past. He flashes to his phone conversation with Sal. *Earth shattering stuff,* he said. *I'd bet my life on it.* The words sound eerily

243

prophetic and equally frightening. His thoughts jumble, blurring together, racing through his head. He's never had a nervous breakdown but wonders if this is what it feels like. He realizes, much to his shame, that he's reached the proverbial breaking point. Fear, guilt, humiliation, pretty much every shitty feeling you can dredge up is raining down on Web like a floodplain storm. He is totally and unequivocally rolling in the muck of regret and remorse, Aldous Huxley's wisdom be damned. It becomes clear to him that he is six feet under. He hopped in the hole all by himself and knows for a fact that he can't climb out. All he's waiting for now is the first spade full of dirt.

When alcoholics finally own up to the fact that they can't live without the bottle it's known as *acceptance*. It's the moment when the healing finally can begin. Web has reached that moment of clarity. He knows what he must now do. He stands and whispers a single name.

"Grace."

47

The minute Web leaves through the front door the back door quietly creaks open. Holly slips inside. She freezes in place, listening. Apparently Pa's wisdom of *go on sound before sight* doesn't just apply to hikes in the deep forest. Convinced she's alone, she pads into her bedroom. She hurriedly stuffs some clothes in her backpack and heads toward the backdoor. Just as she places her hand on the doorknob she pauses, listening again, but also thinking. A thought passes, settles and takes root. Holly quietly walks past the dinette and stops before Web's bedroom door. She gives it an experimental nudge and the squeak of the hinges sounds like a shriek to her in the silence. She reflexively hunkers down and after scolding herself for her overreaction pushes the door open enough for her to slip through.

She stands and takes in the small, exceptionally tidy space. Other than the partially unpacked duffle bag it looks like no one had spent as much as a night there. It's like someone had hung a little hotel doorknob sign asking for turndown service and an overly conscientious, or anal retentive maid had come and gone. Holly half expects to find mints on the pillow.

She steps around the bed and stands before the

duffle bag. She reaches in, not before giving one cursory glance over her shoulder and draws out an overstuffed notebook. It's for his Town of Heroes book. She flips through the notes and transcribed interviews. For a guy Web had surprisingly readable handwriting. She places the notebook back inside the duffle, careful to arrange it as she found it, and rises from her seat on the bed. She smooths out the creases on the bedsheet, made from her sitting there, but as she's drawing her hand over the side edge of the bed she spies something peeking just slightly out from under the mattress. A tiny triangle of paper, like the corner of a slice of cheese poking out from between two slices of bread. She pulls it out and finds it's a large manila envelope full of more notes, almost as many pages of notes as the Town of Heroes notebook. She looks them over, keying on words like Dealey Plaza, November 22nd, 1963, assassination, Oswald, Kennedy. But it's another name that gets her attention: Patience Concannon. She hurriedly puts everything back inside the envelope, slips it under her arm, looks the room over for traces of her visit and eases the door back to its original position before she entered. Holly passes through the main room directly into Pa's bedroom with the manila folder tucked under her arm. When she comes out a second later she's no longer carrying the folder. She heads for the back door. While crossing the room she notices the tape recorder sitting on the table. She picks it up, hits the rewind button and then hits play.

48

In Grace's market, Web tells Grace what happened with Holly and the drifter. Grace nods quietly, showing virtually no emotion during Web's account. *Nothing seems to rattle these people*, Web thinks. You could tell them the world is going to end in ten minutes and they'd probably say 'Well, that still leaves time for a good cup of coffee.'

When he's through Grace takes a deep breath and considers things for a moment. "This fella you shot. Young guy in his twenties, little scruffy, dark hair?"

Web nods.

"Big yellow patch on his right shoulder?"

Web nods again.

Grace shakes her head, satisfied with her conclusion. "Must be that drifter that tried to steal from me." She fixes Web with a steely glare. "You sure this fella was trying to rape Holly?"

"I'm...I'm not sure. It looked like it, but Holly told me..." Web turns his head and rubs at his eyebrow in a subconscious stalling tactic.

"Holly told you what?"

Web turns his eyes back to Grace. "Holly said *she* was attacking *him.*"

247

Grace, under her breath, "Sounds familiar."

Web paces nervously. "I think I may have just killed an innocent man."

Grace steps in front of him, blocking his path. Web draws up short just as Grace slaps him across the face. Hard. Her face is grim, her blue eyes cold, set. "No one is innocent. You got that? Need I remind you that you were a rifleman of the highest order in the United States Marine Corp whose job it was to make split-second decisions in the heat of battle." She waves a hand dismissively in his direction as she turns and walks over to the front windows. She stares out into space. "This was no different." Grace turns back to Web, her voice steely, no nonsense. "There is no room for second guessing. You assessed the situation, made your call and acted. You make your decisions and live with them. No looking back." She takes a step closer and looks even more deeply into his eyes, her voice softening. "You did the right thing." Grace turns her face away, looking over the store like she was assessing it for tax purposes. Her voice shifts, becomes almost casual. "Besides, some people need killing." She wanders away, idly tidying up.

Web is shocked back into speech. "But what if the police come looking?"

Grace throws him a disinterested *yeah, whatever* look and realigns a row of canned peaches. "Even if they did, which I sorely doubt, nothing would come of it." She addresses him a little more sternly again. "What happens in Little Norway stays in Little Norway. Am I clear on that?"

Web is still frozen in stunned silence.

Grace strides purposely over to him and plants her feet square, all business. "We take care of our own. The Unit comes before the individual. Isn't that right, soldier?"

At that moment Web is back on Parris Island, South Carolina, a lowly recruit, just beginning to understand the world he signed up for. He was so fresh off the bus that he still found himself rubbing his newly shaved head because it felt so, well, so weird. Before the Corp he liked to wear it a little long, a little rock star-ish. Drove his dad nuts. Watching it fall off his head in clumps as the base barber shaved it off in shockingly fast, practiced strokes was the first moment Web realized he wasn't in Kansas anymore.

He was about to begin twelve weeks of sledgehammer training designed for one purpose, to break him down to his most basic parts only to be rebuilt as a Marine. It really was like the TV commercials where a piece of raw steel is pounded and shaped until it becomes a saber. Take eighteen year old boys, feed them piles of protein, make them do a million push-ups and hump five miles a day with a fifty pound pack and before long you've got junior grade supermen. And then there's the Crucible. What you simultaneously look forward to and dread for your entire time on the Island. The culmination of all your training poured into one 54-hour stretch of hell. You go in one side a punk-ass kid and come out the other side the most respected individual who walks God's green earth: a Marine.

And the Corp doesn't stop with remolding your body;

more importantly, they remold your character. You're still you, only better. It's every sports cliché you've ever heard, writ large. *There is no 'I' in Team. Give 110%. Win as a team, lose as a team.* Ah yes, The Team. The Corp. The Unit. All come before the individual.

The words snap Web out of his daze. He nods and collapses into a chair by the wall. After a moment he collects himself and looks squarely at Grace. "I was dishonorably discharged." Grace listens, emotionless, giving him her undivided attention. Web actually gives a low chuckle. "Wanna guess how?"

Grace says, "Web Weller, you have finally done it. You have successfully stumped me on matters of the military. For the life of me I cannot imagine how someone of your character could be dishonorably discharged."

"Well, you wouldn't have read about it in the papers or seen it on the Internet. It was need-to-know information and virtually no one was on that receiving list. The short of it is I shot a Ba'ath party member before he could get asylum in the U.S. A Ba'ath party member who helped plan an ambush that killed my brother who was part of a convoy." Web gets a faraway look in his eyes. "The military didn't know we were brothers when they put me on the asylum security detail. Funny, huh? My mission was to keep the bastard safe, but instead I put a round right over his left eyebrow. Imagine my superiors' surprise."

"How'd they not know you were brothers?"

"Same father, different mothers. My brother took his mom's maiden name to keep her family name going. That's the kind of son he was." Web stares at his shoes, fidgets a bit. "I suppose that's why my dad was always so much more devoted to him."

Grace says, "It's hard to imagine the military missing something like that."

Web shakes his head. "Not really. I've had doctors send me wrong test results; I've received bills that were incorrect. It was a clerical error. Slipped through the cracks. The U.S. Military has a lot of moving parts and occasionally mistakes get made."

"You'd think your father would be proud of you for avenging your brother's death."

"The military didn't tell him. When they realized their fuck up..."

Grace finishes his thought. "They dummied up. It was an embarrassment so it became officially classified. Hush, hush."

Web responds by tapping the tip of his nose to indicate she nailed it.

Grace nods at the revelation. "They were pissed at you. You made them look bad. Thus, the dishonorable discharge."

Web matches her nod.

"And that's why the letters to your father keep coming back," Grace continues. "He still doesn't know. To him you're just the dishonorably discharged son."

Web looks up from under his eyes, embarrassed.

"So why didn't you ever tell your father you took the shot?"

"I dunno. Guess cuz I'm too damn stubborn. I've thought of telling him a million times and a million times

251

I've changed my mind. I tell myself I shouldn't have to justify my actions just to earn his love. I figure I'll tell him eventually. Whether he believes me or not...well, we'll see."

Grace puts a hand on Web's shoulder and gives him a tender kiss on the cheek. And then with a subtle grin, she gives him a quiet Marine... "Oohrah."

49

Evening settles over Little Norway like wet wool. A low cloud cover brings the fringes of darkness early. Web takes his time making the walk back to Pa's house. Six blocks of crushed and oiled rock make up Shire Street. Pa's house is the only one on the road, located up at the end where it rises up before the landscape turns feral. There are only a handful of roads in Little Norway. The avenues run north-south, the streets east-west, just like Manhattan. The four avenues, 1st through 4th, bracket Grace's market. Erickson Street, home to the Cabin, the cemetery, and the Evangelical Lutheran Church of America (starring Pastor Gladstone "Gladdy" Merrill, he of the mellifluous baritone) runs behind the market. Shire Street branches off the highway, directly from the front doors of the market. In other words Grace's market is sort of the nerve center of Little Norway. Web had asked Grace how Shire Street got its name. One of the city fathers a big Lord of the Rings fan? A literary nod to J.R.R. Tolkien's home of the Hobbits? The truth wasn't nearly as romantic.

"Ol' Fred Shire, town drunk way back in ought seven," explained Grace. "He lived on the exact opposite side of town, in a shack out behind the cemetery. Where the market stands now is where one of the town watering holes used to be, The Black Beagle, it was called, on account of the owner's peculiarly colored hound. This was back when there were more drinking establishments in Little Norway than, well, pert near any other business. Well, Fred—for some reason that no one could ever put a finger on—whenever he left the Beagle, instead of heading west to his home he always ended up staggering east. Back then the road wasn't much more than a wide trail folks used when heading off into the woods. It didn't matter how many times Fred left the Beagle he always turned left when he should have been turning right. Something about his internal GPS was all screwy. It became such a common occurrence that the trail eventually got dubbed Shire Street in Fred's honor."

So much for dignified history.

Unlike the street's namesake Web makes the walk stone sober, although his confession to Grace leaves him feeling slightly out-of-body, like he's tossed back a pint or two.

Web strides up the last steps to Pa's house and steps though the front door. There's a small fire in the fireplace to his left giving the room a shadowy soft orange glow that flickers and shifts. The room is dead quiet other than the occasional pop and sizzle from the fire. Web listens to the silence for a moment before offering up a low "Pa?"

From a dim corner of the room, quietly..."I'm right here."

Web turns to see Pa sitting silently in his overstuffed chair, his rifle across his lap, the barrel reflecting a dull gleam from the fire.

Web squints Pa's way. "You okay, Pa?"

Pa, perfectly still, "How far was the shot? On the drifter."

Pa's demeanor, his stillness spring Web's sniper instincts into high alert. He considers the question for a moment before answering as passively as possible. "Maybe six hundred yards."

Web thinks he catches a glimpse of a smile form on Pa's lips but it may simply be a trick of the shifting firelight.

Pa's stillness is utter and complete. He might as well be a waxworks dummy for his lack of movement. If Web didn't see his lips move he'd swear the chair was holding a corpse.

The lips move again. "That's a good shot." After a beat..."Felt good, didn't it?"

Web nods.

Finally movement from the chair, if even infinitesimal, a simple tip down of the head, maybe half an inch, and back up. Too subtle to be considered a proper nod but enough to telegraph approval.

Pa says, "That reminds me." One of his hands comes off the rifle, reaching into a pants pocket and rummaging for a second before returning with something held between his thumb and forefinger. Something flat and black. He tosses it to Web. "Here, a little something."

Web catches the object instinctively. He looks it over in the dim light. It's the drifter's knife, still warm from Pa's pocket.

Pa rumbles, "I was never much on souvenirs but when

you crack off a particularly good shot it's nice to have something to remember it by. You earned it."

Neither man says anything. The silence hanging thick between them, then, from the chair, so quietly it can barely register in Web's ears, "Bastard got what was coming."

Web steps further into the space, slowly, cautiously. His eyes flick around the room, taking in all corners, like a cop entering an unfamiliar apartment and expecting an ambush. Web's eyes go back to Pa. "I know. I couldn't let Holly get hurt."

A sound, almost like the start of a laugh begins and is extinguished nearly as fast. "I'm not talking about that punk with Holly."

Web freezes, not sure how to answer.

Pa continues, even more quietly, "Used her and threw her aside. My beautiful Helen."

There's a moment in the second Star Wars movie, *The Empire Strikes Back*, where Darth Vader tells Luke Skywalker that he's Luke's father. At that precise moment back in 1980 every person in the theater went, "*What the hell did he just say?*" and their minds raced back to the first movie and within seconds the clouds parted, the light bulb went on and the puzzle pieces fell together.

Web is experiencing that same flash of recognition all over again. He speaks to Pa quietly, neutrally. "She became an inconvenience, an embarrassment, so they had her killed to keep her quiet."

There's no response for a moment, just the quiet crackling of the fire. Finally from Pa, "No, it was just an accident."

Pa lets out a low, soft breath. Not quite a sigh but definitely from the same family. Web detects a shift in the chair, a subtle back and forth motion and hears the corresponding squeaks, like Pa is nestling deeper into the cushions, settling, like an old house.

"They were slipping her out of the White House through one of those tunnels you've heard about. It was winter." Pa is actually smiling softly but there's no warmth in it.

"Those tunnels aren't as glamorous as the rumors let on. They're dank, the ceilings leak." Pa gives a shrug. "A puddle of water, leather sole pumps..." Pa's eyes drift to the fire. "Strapless with an open toe, her favorites. She slipped. Back of her head split right open on the concrete." Pa's eyes round back on Web. "An accident, pure and simple."

"How do you know all this?"

"My specialty was reconnaissance. This was just another mission, except it was personal. I needed to find out, so I found out."

"And so you blamed the President for her death."

For the first time Pa's voice takes on volume and edge. "If he hadn't seduced her she wouldn't have been in that tunnel in the first place. From where I'm sitting he was as guilty as the day is long and he paid the price."

Web fixes Pa with an even stare. "So you shot him. You killed the President."

Pa actually smiles at this. A chilled smile. The kind that raise goosebumps when you're on the receiving end.

"That would make a good story, wouldn't it? Something a publisher would jump at."

Web feels his blood pressure drop a notch. "What are you talking about?"

Pa holds up a thick manila envelope that had been leaning against the side of the chair, lost in the shadows. The orange glow from the fireplace flickers across the surface. There's no mistaking it. It's the one Web had hidden under his mattress, stuffed full of all his notes, his research.

When Web's mom's doctor first told him his mother had cancer it was like someone had kicked the legs out from under his chair and thrown a bucket of ice water on him. That same disorientation and sudden wave of cold washes over Web at that instant but he manages to keep his voice surprisingly calm, even to his own ears. "Where did you find that?"

Pa tips his head to one side. "Who shot President Kennedy? Do you really know, Web? It's been a bit of a controversy all these years, hasn't it? So tell me, who shot President Kennedy?"

"Pa, stop it."

Pa responds by slowly rising up from his chair, his rifle clutched in front of him. "Who shot Kennedy?"

Web eases away. His heel catches on the fireplace poker leaning against the hearth and knocks it down. One end lands in the fire, kicking up a cloud of angry sparks between the two men. "C'mon, Pa, now just settle down."

Pa is now yelling. "Dammit, who shot Kennedy?!! Tell me!"

Web yells back. "You did!"

Silence.

Pa stares back, the barrel of his gun drops and he says evenly, "Maybe you're right." He turns and walks back to his chair, speaking over his shoulder, "But maybe I didn't kill him."

A new voice joins in from behind Web. "Maybe he had help."

Web turns to see Grace standing on the front door threshold.

Web looks back and forth between Grace and Pa. "I don't understand."

Grace says matter of factly, "Everyone talks about the lone gunman theory. Who says it had to be a man?"

Web fumbles with a response. "I'm...it's just..."

Grace arches an eyebrow in his direction. "You saying a woman couldn't have made the shot?"

Web, feeling like he's back in third grade standing before he principal shakes his head slowly, deliberately. "No, Ma'am."

Grace nods in return. Not a crack of a smile. "Damn straight."

Web regains his footing. "So are you telling me..."

But Grace holds a hand up, cutting him off. "Web, do not ask questions you do not want answers to. Instead let's play a game called *What If?*"

Pa chimes in. "Suppose the first shot came in low, went through Kennedy's throat, hit Governor Connolly in the front seat. Shot wouldn't have been fatal to the President."

Grace says, "Maybe the second shot was rushed.

Missed completely."

Web continues the thought. "So a third, fatal shot would suggest a spectacularly quick breech and fire or..." Web turns back to face Grace. "...a two gun team."

Pa says, "When you need to be sure."

Grace steps further into the room. "And suppose you were part of that two gun team?"

Web is visibly shifting into mission mode. "I'd place the first shooter in the Texas School Book Depository."

Pa nods. "Just like Oswald."

Web says, "Or maybe a similar building. Rear angle, high ground, target moving slowly away in a straight line."

Pa nods. "Tactically sound."

Web nods back then continues. "Second gun..."

Pa interrupts him. "If there *was* a second gun."

Web acknowledges this and continues with his theory. "Same side but from the front, triangulating, split the eyewitness accounts."

Pa says, "Maybe the grassy knoll."

Web shakes his head. "Too close; you could be spotted, doesn't offer ready escape. If it were me I'd set up camp at the railway overpass to the north. Good escape routes, prime coverage, damn tough angle though. Long distance." Web looks to Grace. "That would take a hell of a shot."

Grace quietly nods, "Yes, it would."

Web says, "The final consideration would have to be diversion: drawing attention to something or someone else. Finding a patsy." Web turns back to Pa. "But it would take some serious inside intelligence to know an ex-military personnel with a communist background; a perfect fall guy, who happened to own a certain type of Italian rifle, was going to be in the Texas School Book Depository the day of the shooting."

Pa says, "Or a simpler explanation: that ex-military personnel with a communist background really *was* the shooter."

Web says, "But that wouldn't make for a good story, would it?"

Pa holds up the manila envelope. "Which brings us back to why we're all gathered here in the first place."

Web doesn't flinch. He's still in mission mode. "I never submitted anything."

At this moment Holly quietly steps out of the shadows with her own rifle. Her hair is scattered about her head like a tangle of barbed wire. Her eyes are the epitome of *if looks could kill.*

"He's lying." She holds up his tape recorder and hits the play button. Web's conversation with Sal spills out of the small, tinny speaker. It's all there: his offer to Sal of an earth-shattering story. Holly clicks off the recorder, her words directed at Pa, but her eyes never leaving Web. "Pa, he don't give a damn about you or me or anyone else in this town. He only cares about one thing, to get his story published and his name in the headlines. You just watch, he'll get his precious story published and then he'll be gone, leave us in the dust."

Web, perfectly stoic, says, "That's not true."

Holly springs forward quickly, bringing her rifle to

bear on him. "Liar!" She looks frantically to Pa and Grace. "He has no honor! You can see that, right?" Holly turns her attention back to Web. "I can take care of it right now. One shot and we'll be back to the way it was before he showed up. When it was just me and Pa." She brings the rifle up a little higher, aimed a little more at Web's head. "What happens in Little Norway stays in Little Norway." Holly circles over a little closer to Pa, keeping the rifle still trained on Web. "You're going to sell Pa out! Say it! I want to hear you admit it, so Pa can see you for the shit that you are. Say it!"

Grace quietly steps forward. "How do you know Web was talking about Pa? Maybe it's something else entirely."

Holly's jaw drops open like a trapdoor on a loose hinge. "Are you serious? How can you stand up for this scum?"

Pa raises a hand from his gun, his finger in the air, *A moment, please* signal. He speaks quietly. "Holly..."

But Holly's anger is at the wheel and it's not interested in making any stops. "No, Pa, this son of a bitch..."

"Enough!" The single word bursts forth from Pa with such power and finality that Holly not only shuts up, she actually takes a step back as if an iron door slammed in her face.

Pa lets the silence hang there for a moment before speaking again. His words back to their previous quiet rumble. "Whatever Web may have done, whatever he may be, whatever will come of this evening the one thing you will take from all this is that he may very well have saved your life. You'd best remember that."

Holly's anger, temporarily doused by Pa's outburst still smolders. Her words creep out from deep in her throat. Almost a growl. "I don't believe it."

Web's eye dart from Holly to Pa but he remains silent. He himself would like to know what the hell Pa is talking about.

Pa's hand goes back down, settling on the rifle again. "That boy, the one Web shot, he was a bad one."

Holly's eyes flash back and forth between Pa and Web, unsure of what she's hearing. "What are you talking about?"

Pa calmly continues, but his words are still dark. "Trent David Clemons. Most recent address, Washington State penitentiary, Walla Walla, Washington. Released six months ago after serving a two years sentence for sexual assault. A criminal record as long as my arm and currently wanted by authorities on suspicion of assault."

Web blurts out... "But how..."

Pa says, "He was carrying ID." Pa shakes his head sadly or perhaps more out of disgust. "Typical criminal. Not the sharpest tool."

"But...but I shot him...less than twelve hours ago. How..."

Pa cuts him off again, his words short, curt, like someone who's fed up with having to explain himself and whose patience is wearing thin. "I. Find. Things."

A loud snap from the fire acts like an exclamation point to Pa's words before silence once again envelops the room.

When Web looks to Pa he sees, what, regret? Or worse,

disappointment? On Holly he sees something etched much more clearly. You can travel all over the world and no matter where you open your Samsonite there's no mistaking cold, remorseless hate. If Pa's words had an effect on Holly she's keeping any change of heart under lock and key.

The players in the drama are still as ice. Finally Grace breaks the stalemate. She looks to Web. "Web, listen to me. I want you to go to the market and stay there until I come for you. Lucia Tolborg's watching it for me. Tell her I'll be there shortly."

Holly erupts. "What?!"

But Web doesn't budge. "No."

Grace turns on him with deadly seriousness. "Web, get your ass over to the store right this minute." She pauses, softens, and says, "Besides, you have a guest waiting for you."

Web looks confused by this last comment, but after a moment he slowly edges toward the door.

Holly jumps forward with her rifle. "You take one more step and I'll blow you to hell and back. I don't care what Pa says about that guy in the woods, it still doesn't take away from the fact that you're still a lying sack of shit who's looking to sell us out!"

Grace steps in front of the rifle, without taking her eyes off of Holly, "Web. Go. Now."

Web deliberately turns his back on Holly's rifle and walks out the door. Once outside he hurries to his Lincoln, jumps in with the roof down, keys it, slams it into gear and speeds away down the road.

Back inside Holly sprints across the room. "You don't understand! I have to stop him; he's going to leave; he's going to tell!" Holly bursts past Grace, knocking her aside and sprints out the door.

Holly runs down the road, cutting off to the right to scurry up an embankment with a view of Shire Street heading off toward town. From her vantage point she can see Web's car rumbling down the road away from her. She sights down the Lincoln with her scope, Web's head in the crosshairs. She cocks the bolt-action rifle and snugs the gun to her shoulder.

Riflescopes are like magic. Light passes through the lens at the far end, known as the objective lens and focuses on a point inside the scope. The lens at the near end, the ocular lens, magnifies the light from that focal point. When you look through the scope what you're seeing—your target—is actually that light being let in. You're looking at an image created purely of light. Though it's dark on Shire Street there's still enough illumination seeping through the clouds to offer a view. You wouldn't want to read by it without your cheaters but it's good enough for government work. At that moment the light passing through the scope is in the form of Web's head, silhouetted against the beam of his headlights splashed on the crushed rock road in front of him.

But the angle's wrong. From Holly's perspective she would be seeing the back-right side of Web's head. There would be no silhouette because there would be nothing but dark forest behind him.

The view from this scope is directly from behind.

The crosshairs hold on Web's skull for the briefest of moments but then the sight pans right. The crosshairs come to rest on Holly.

50

Holly slows her breathing. She's kneeling; her left elbow propped on her left knee like a tripod. Web's head fills her scope. Her finger begins to tighten on the trigger... and everything before her eyes explodes.

The impact of the bullet shears Holly's scope in two while at the same time shattering it, sending bits of glass, aluminum and plastic bursting outward in all directions, including into Holly's stunned face. Her finger reflexively pulls the trigger, but the gun barrel is now pointing somewhere a good several degrees higher. Her shot harmlessly clips a tree branch above the Lincoln. At the sound of the two shots Web's head snaps around but there is nothing to see in the failing light and no evident damage. The car drives on.

51

Grace lowers Pa's rifle from her shoulder as Pa steps up beside her. He rests a hand softly on her arm and offers a single word. "Thanks."

52

Web walks into the market and finds Sal Shelby
flirting with Lucia Tolborg. She's a pretty young thing,
close to Holly's age, but decidedly more teenagery. All
elbows and knees, her dishwater blonde hair tied back
with a scrunchie, she's chewing gum and trying to look
coy. She's clearly enjoying the attention heaped upon her
by Sal. When she sees Web come in she gets embarrassed,
afraid she's doing something wrong. Probably afraid
Web's going to rat her out to Gracie.

When Sal turns to see Web a big smile comes over him.
"Geez, they serve all kinds here."

Web isn't in the mood for cute banter. His instincts tell
him he just dodged a bullet, both figuratively and literally,
and can't for the life of him understand why he's still
standing. He takes his confusion and fear out on the man
in front of him. "Sal, what the hell are you doing here?"

Sal's head jerks back in mock surprise. "No, no, all
wrong. See, I say, "Geez, they serve all kinds here", and
you say something like, 'Obviously. You're here, aren't
you?' That's called clever banter between friends."

The Sally social magic at work. Web cracks a smile.
"Sorry, you just surprised me." Web turns to Lucia. "You
can go now, Lucia. Grace said I can watch the place 'til

271

she gets back."

Lucia nods and shuffles out the front door without a word.

Sal watches her leave. "I can see why you've stuck around here, Web. These people are a riot."

Web says, "Scandinavian stoicism. It's kind of an acquired taste."

The two men exchange a quick man-hug, the kind where they grasp hands like they're arm wrestling and draw each other in for a quick pat on the back with the free arm.

At that moment the front door opens and Pa, Grace and Holly enter. Pa and Holly are all furrowed brows and tight lips. The physical definition of grim. But Grace is all smiles, acting like everything's peaches and cream.

"Web, my dear boy, thanks for minding the store." Grace turns to face Sal with an appraising look. "And who is this handsome friend of yours?"

Web makes tentative introductions all around while keeping constant eye contact with Grace. He's still holding onto his veneer of control but it's fragile at best. Grace ignores his stare, still all small town charm.

"So, Mr. Sal Shelby, world famous author, and hob-nobber of the hoi polloi, what brings you to our little slice of heaven?" While she asks this she casually walks around behind the counter like she's just going back to work.

Holly, her eyes flashing to Grace, eases herself away from Sal.

Sal, slipping into cocktail party mode, returns the smile and gives a nod in Web's direction. "Well, my good friend Web here convinced me that he had a great story to tell. Something to pass along to my publisher, and who am I to pass up a great story?" And then, with a polished smirk, "Especially if I can get a cut of the profits." Sal steps over and puts a fraternal arm around Web's shoulder. "He sounded so convincing that I couldn't bring myself to sit around and wait so I just grabbed a flight out here."

Grace says, "So your publisher paid for you to come all the way out here just for the possibility of a great story? Where can I get a job like that?"

Sal scrunches his face up. "Paid for me? That cheapskate? No, he doesn't even know anything about this. Hell, no one does. I just took off on the spur of the moment."

Grace slaps a hand on the counter top. "Boy-Howdy! Web, you have a true friend here in Sal. The man has, for all intents and purposes, dropped off the face of the planet just to visit you." Still smiling she says, "Gracious, he could fall into a hole and no one would even know where he was." Grace and Sal get a laugh out of this. No one else is laughing. While she's laughing Grace's hands drop below the counter. Behind the counter Grace's rifle is on a shelf mere inches below her hands. Pa glances nervously at Grace but she ignores him. "So, Web, what is this earth shattering story that you can't wait to tell the world about?"

Web doesn't miss a beat. He turns to Sal, all business. "I wasn't lying, it's a big story." Web turns away and walks over to lean against the wall. He's standing directly under the Mannlicher-Carcano rifle. "One that will shake people all the way to the top."

Sal smiles back and forth between Web and Grace. "I'm all ears."

Pa eases closer to Holly. Web turns to look at Grace. Grace's hands are now touching the rifle behind the counter.

Web says, "It's the story..." Web turns back to Sal and walks briskly toward him. "...of a U.S. military officer selling innocent women into the sex slave trade."

Holly's eyes flash to Grace. Pa nods understandingly. Grace's empty hands come up to rest on the counter.

Sal's eyebrows shoot up. "Are you serious? That's dynamite stuff! You weren't kidding when you said it was money."

Web says, "It was a long time ago. Classified."

"I don't care if it happened pre-Jurassic, it's still huge!"

"It's just one of the many stories I've been compiling from veterans here in Little Norway. There are other stories, maybe not as sexy but just as powerful. It'll be part of a book called A Town of Heroes."

Sal rubs his hands together. "Can't wait to read it," then promptly snaps out his cell phone. "I'm gonna call my publisher right now." Sal steps away and starts dialing. While he's dialing, "Anything else you been working on?"

Web calmly looks toward Grace. "One more thing. Has to do with the Kennedy assassination." Pa and Holly stiffen. Grace's hands ease back behind the counter.

Sal looks at his phone; the call was dropped. "Cheap ass phone." He starts dialing again. Sal, preoccupied with his dialing, glances up at Web. "Kennedy? That sounds promising. What is it?"

Web says, "It's the story of the real assassin."

At this moment Grace brings the rifle up in a flash and yells, "Sal!"

When Sal turns to see Grace holding the rifle his eyes go wide. The room is silent for a beat, then Sal quietly says, "Is...that a Johnson Arms 1941?"

Grace is all smiles. "Web said you were a collector of old guns. Thought you might like to take a look at it."

Sal forgets his phone call and strides over to see the gun. "She's a beauty. Probably worth around $6,000. You interested in selling it?"

"I'll think about it."

While admiring the gun Sal asks Web, "So what's this Kennedy thing you were talking about? Real assassin? What, conspiracy theory stuff? Fiction?"

Web, his eyes on Grace, cracks a sly smile. "Yeah, of course, fiction."

Sal, oblivious to the tension in the room continues his admiration of the old gun. "Nah, my guy doesn't do fiction." Sal remembers his phone, snaps it open and starts dialing again.

Grace moves out from behind the counter and steps over to Web and Pa. She locks eyes with Web and quietly asks, "Do you believe what Pa and I told you earlier at his house?"

Web looks back innocently. "You mean that stuff about a pair of backwoods hicks assassinating the President of the United States of America? Who would believe it?"

Web waits a beat then continues. "Besides, every sane person knows it was Oswald. Or the mob. Or Castro. Or the CIA. You know, the reasonable explanations."

At this moment the front door swings open with a ring of the bell and a middle-aged man dressed in blue enters, his hands clutching a small bundle of mail. "Sorry about getting here so late, Grace. Had some truck trouble."

Graces steps over and takes the letters from the carrier. "Not a problem, Cliff. Say hi to Bernice and the kids for me." The mailman leaves, setting off another tinkling of the bell above the door. Grace absentmindedly glances through the letters while Sal turns excitedly toward the group.

"My publisher can't wait to see your stuff, Web. He wants to know how soon you can fly to New York to make your pitch?"

"Give me a day or two."

Sal babbles something short into his phone and snaps it shut before turning to Web, his arms opened wide. "Congratulations, Web, you did it! You finally got what you've been hoping for!" Sal races over to give Web a hug. The real kind this time with lots of backslapping, hoots and hollers. Pa adds into the mix, a smile from ear to ear. Even Holly manages to make eye contact. She leans in close to Web and whispers in his ear, "I take it back. Everything. You're an honorable man." She leans in farther, lightly touching her forehead to his and rests it there for a beat.

Through all of this Grace is focused on one of the

letters that have just been delivered. She glances up at the celebration then back down again at the letter, her face a mask. In the upper left corner of the envelope, the place reserved for the return address and sender Grace fixes on a name. Nicholas Weller. Her eyes come back up again; her mouth bends in a smile.

THE END

AUTHOR BRYAN JOHNSTON

Bryan has been a television and video writer/producer for nearly three decades during which he has won 10 Emmys along with several other national awards. He is the author of three books and has written for numerous magazines and websites. He was also blessed with being an on-air movie reviewer for ten years--according to Bryan the greatest gig on the planet.

He currently lives in Lake Forest Park, Washington, just outside of Seattle with his wife, two kids and two very large dogs. He is a devout movie lover, sports fan and avid reader. He hopes the Seattle Mariners make it to the World Series before he dies, he's been playing competitive softball since Hector was a pup, and he's a mediocre golfer.

ACKNOWLEDGEMENTS

I'd like to acknowledge all the fine people who helped me in this labor of love. First of all, I thank my wife and kids for tolerating me creeping off to my office night after night to endlessly write and rewrite. I want to thank the following servicemen who lent me their expertise. This book is a work of fiction but I wanted to make sure I had my facts straight. Ramon F. Reiser, SFC Ret. (Former Army Sniper and Medic—Big Red 1), Hans Halberstadt (Military Author), Lamar Taylor (Section Leader [Sgt. e-5]—4th Marine Scout Snipers—Viet Nam), Bob Himrod, SFC Ret. (Army Infantry Scout Dog Handler and Member of Counter-Sniper Team), Ben McCall Sgt. E-5 Ret. (Marine Sniper). I would also like to thank my publisher, Kristen Morris, from Tigress Publishing, for working so hard to bring this book to print in record time. Lastly I'd like to thank all my family and friends who helped create many of the memories and experiences I drew from to write this book.